The Miraculous Makeover
OF LIZARD
FLANAGAN

CAROL GORMAN

The Miraculous Makeover
OF LIZARD FLANAGAN

HarperCollins*Publishers*

Many thanks to Amy Lemen, Dwight Codr,
Sheila and Calaneet Balas,
and Ben Johnson for their help

The Miraculous Makeover of Lizard Flanagan
Copyright © 1994 by Carol Gorman

Library of Congress Cataloging-in-Publication Data
Gorman, Carol
The miraculous makeover of Lizard Flanagan / Carol Gorman.
    p.   cm.
Summary: As she enters middle school, athletic eleven-year-old Lizard is
dismayed to see her friends change into weird strangers and struggles with
her own transition from tomboy to "girly-girl."
ISBN 0-06-024463-1. — ISBN 0-06-024464-X (lib. bdg.)
[1. Sex role—Fiction.   2. Schools—Fiction.   3. Friendship—Fiction.]
I. Title.
PZ7.G6693Mo   1994   94-1279
[Fic]—dc20   CIP
                                                                     AC

Typography by Al Cetta
1   2   3   4   5   6   7   8   9   10
❖
First Edition

To my editor, Ginee Seo,
with thanks for her patience, enthusiasm,
and terrific ideas

1

"Lizard Flanagan!" yelled my friend Mary Ann Powers. "Hurry up! We're going to be late!"

It was the first day of school, and Mary Ann was waiting for me at the footbridge over the ravine.

I looked at the watch that I'd gotten for my eleventh birthday. (It was a beaut—it had a chronograph with an eight-lap memory for timing races and stuff.) "What are you talking about?" I hollered to Mary Ann. "It's only seven thirty-two in the A.M. We've got almost a half hour until they open the prison doors!"

"But I want to get there early," Mary Ann said.

That gave me an idea, and I sprinted the rest of the way to the bridge. "Maybe we can get up a game of football before the first bell."

Mary Ann didn't say anything.

"I told Sam to tell Zach and Ed and Stinky that we'd be walking because my bike's in the shop. I said we'd meet them at the flagpole. They'll be up for a quick game, I bet. I've got my second-best ball in my backpack; I'm going to keep it in my locker."

Mary Ann stayed quiet.

"So what do you think?" I said. "You up for one last game before the drudgery starts?"

"Well, I'm not really dressed for sports," she said, turning away and starting off toward school.

It was only then, when she walked away from me, that I noticed what she was wearing. A short denim skirt, a red-and-white print blouse, and flat dress shoes. I couldn't believe it. The last time I'd seen Mary Ann wear a skirt to school was in third grade when she dressed up as a witch for the Halloween parade, and she wore a long, black skirt of her mother's, safety-pinned at the waist to hold it up.

I scowled. "A *skirt*?" I hurried to catch up. "Aren't you going a little overboard?"

Mary Ann bit her lower lip the way she

2

always does when she gets self-conscious. "Well, gee, it's the first day of middle school," she said. "I thought I should dress up a little."

"You think you're a *little* dressed up?" I said. "No, Mary Ann, *I'm* a little dressed up." I looked down at my shorts (new this summer), my favorite Chicago Cubs T-shirt (not a stain on it), my Adidas running shoes (no holes), and then I looked at her. "*You're* dressed for a wedding."

"Oh, for Pete's sake," she said. "I am not." She leaned over, midstride, and scratched her leg where a mosquito had bitten her yesterday.

I glanced down at her leg, then stopped her.

"*Hose?*" I said, touching her knee with all the scab scars. "You're wearing panty hose? Are you nuts? It's going to be eighty-five degrees this afternoon, and Truman Middle School isn't even air-conditioned."

"They're not panty hose, they're tights," Mary Ann corrected me. "And I'll probably survive."

"I didn't even know you owned a pair."

"Lots of people own tights," she said.

"I don't even know where you *get* them," I said.

"A department store."

I shook my head. I couldn't figure out what

had gotten into Mary Ann.

She and I are a lot alike and agree on almost everything, like our Favorite Ice Cream: rocky road; our Most Hated Chore: washing dishes; our Favorite Baseball Team: the Chicago Cubs; and our Worst Nightmare: having to go to school during the summer.

And we never dress up. Ever.

We were the only girls in our class at Washington Elementary School who played in the metro baseball and flag football leagues, or climbed trees, or caught frogs down at the creek. In other words, we're the only girls at school who had any fun.

We've always hung out with the guys: my twin brother Sam, Zach Walters, Ed Mechtensteimer, and Stinky Porter. They're the best friends anybody could have. They're fun, they like baseball and football, and they know how to have a good time.

The girls are another story. You wouldn't believe what they do for fun. Heather Parks and Jennifer Wilkes and Tiffany Brady and some of the others spend hours polishing their nails and curling their hair. They have big slumber parties where they read beauty magazines and try out new hairstyles and talk about boys.

I can't believe they do such boring stuff and *like* it.

Mary Ann and I always said we'd rather spit into the wind than act as stupid as those girls. So I couldn't believe that Mary Ann, one of my very best friends, was standing here in front of me all dressed up and wearing *panty hose*, for crying out loud.

I could see she wasn't about to change her mind, though. Besides, it was probably too late for her to run home and get normal anyway. So I figured we'd better start walking. I knew she was going to be hot and miserable in those panty hose. That would teach her.

"Come on," I said. "Let's go."

Truman Middle School is on the edge of town, and a lot of the kids take buses or come in car pools. Mary Ann and I usually ride our bikes with the guys, but since my bike was getting fixed, she had said she'd walk with me today.

We got there before the buses did and leaned up against the big ash tree near the circular drive and watched the kids arrive. The familiar faces belonged to kids who'd been in our class at Washington Elementary. I recognized some who'd gone to Wash ahead of us who were now seventh and eighth graders. A few of

5

them hardly looked like the same people, they'd changed so much since elementary school.

Mostly, though, I watched the new faces, the kids from Mark Twain and Jefferson elementary schools.

I nudged Mary Ann. "There's Al Pickering. He was a great quarterback for the Cougars last year."

"Where?" said Mary Ann. "Don't point. Just tell me where he is."

"You can't miss him," I said. "He's wearing a purple T-shirt, and he's looking over this way. Hi!" I waved and Al waved back.

"Now he knows we're talking about him!" Mary Ann whispered, turning her back to him. Her cheeks turned pink.

"So what?" I said. "He's a great guy. Don't you remember? He and I QB'ed when the Raiders played the Cougars last year."

"Sure, I remember," she said, smiling. "The Raiders were awesome. We won that game."

"Just barely, remember? I sneaked through that hole in the defense and scored that touchdown in the last five seconds of the game."

"Yeah," Mary Ann said, grinning. "I was wide open in the end zone, but you decided to take it in yourself!"

I stared at her. "Wide open, are you

kidding! Guys were all over you!"

"That's not the way I remember it." She was still smiling.

That's Mary Ann. She likes pulling my chain.

"You're full of it, Mary Ann," I said. "Just ask Zach about that last play."

"He'd side with you no matter what you said."

"Yeah, 'cause he knows I'm right!"

Football is a lot of fun, but baseball's my specialty. Mary Ann's, too. In the metro leagues, the positions get passed around a lot to give everyone a chance to do what they like best. But I have to say that when I pitched last year, we won more than we lost. I have a great curveball. Mary Ann and I—and the rest of the guys—are going out for the middle-school baseball team next spring. The Truman Tigers need a good pitcher.

I tapped her arm. "There's Josh Clinton and Ben Peterson from the Warriors. They broke league records for hitting last year."

"Some of these kids look really *old*," Mary Ann said. "Check out that girl in the white shorts. She looks sixteen."

"Yeah," I said. "Probably an eighth grader."

"She looks so sophisticated."

Most of the girls were dressed like Mary Ann, in skirts or dressy walking shorts. I didn't examine any other legs closely, but I think there were more than a few pairs of panty hose walking around in the heat that morning.

My brother Sam arrived with Zach and Ed and Stinky on their bikes.

"Hey, Sam! Zach!" I yelled.

The guys looked over and grinned. They locked their bikes to the rack and came over. Zach punched me on the arm. "No more freedom," he said. "We're prisoners for nine long months, Lizard."

A girl standing close by looked over at me and frowned, mouthing my name: *Lizard.* She looked at her friend and they laughed.

That didn't bother me. I get that a lot. I mean, Lizard is a pretty unusual name. Of course, it's not my real name. Mom and Dad named me Elizabeth, and when Sam was two, he couldn't say that. It came out more like "Lizard," and the name stuck. It's a fine name, I think. It sure beats the heck out of Elizabeth.

"What group are you in?" Zach asked.

"Orange," I said.

His face fell. "I'm in the black one. I was hoping we'd get into the same group."

"Yeah. Me, too."

The Truman mascot is a tiger, so every grade is divided into two groups with tiger colors, orange and black. All the kids in one group have the same teachers and move through their classes together. We were sent letters almost a week ago telling us which group we'd be in. Within an hour of the mail delivery that day, we all knew who was in what group. Except for Zach. He was on a fishing trip with his dad.

"Ed and Stinky are in your group," he said.

"I know. Mary Ann and Sam are in yours," I said.

Zach looked into the sky. "I guess it's just as well," he said. He had that look in his eyes that always comes before one of his stories.

"What do you mean?"

"There was a school on the other side of the state," he said. "It was taken over by alien invaders. The aliens marched everybody down to the gym, then divided the kids into two groups, just like our orange and black groups. Made them stand across the gym from each other. Then the aliens told the kids they were going to play basketball. Every kid had to participate in one play of the game. The losing team would have to go with the aliens back to their planet."

By this time, Sam, Mary Ann, Ed, and Stinky were leaning in to hear. No one ever gave up a chance to hear one of Zach's stories.

"Half the school had to go with the aliens?" Ed said. He was grinning, but he was listening hard.

Stinky snorted. "How was there room on the spaceship?"

"They could shrink people to the size of a golf tee," Zach said.

"So what happened?" I said.

"The game went on all afternoon. The aliens said each quarter would be thirty minutes long. Every kid played as if his life depended on it, and of course, it did. First, one team was ahead. Then the other. At the end of the final quarter, with the game tied up and five seconds left on the clock, my cousin Wally stood on the free-throw line. He knew his life depended on the next few seconds.

"Then he looked across the room and saw his best friend on the other team. He didn't know what to do. If his team won, his friend would have to go with the aliens. If his team lost, *he'd* have to go."

"What did he do?" Mary Ann asked.

"He threw the ball. It arced, and came clean through the basket. The game was over. Wally's best friend and the other half of the school had to get shrunk and go with the aliens." Zach looked at me. "So you see, with the six of us divided between the orange and black groups, we're pretty evenly matched." He grinned. "We'd have a great game, wouldn't we?"

Zach loved telling stories as much as we loved hearing them.

"Well, I just want to know one thing," Stinky said.

We turned to him.

"If people are made that small, they'd shrink right out of their clothes. Did the aliens take them all back *naked*?"

We all laughed, and Ed put Stinky in a headlock and rapped his knuckles on Stinky's head while he yowled.

I looked over Zach's shoulder and saw some girls staring at us.

"I think we're being watched," I murmured.

Zach looked back at the girls. All of them laughed and squealed and turned the other way. Except for one girl. She stood tall, her long, wavy blond hair blowing behind her shoulders in the breeze. She was beautiful. She gazed straight at Zach, smiling slightly.

"What's with them?" I said.

"I think they like you, Walters," Sam said, giving Zach a little shove.

"Yeah, right." Zach grinned and shoved Sam back. He glanced over again at the girls, who squealed louder this time. He shrugged and then turned back to me. "When do you get your bike out of the shop?"

"Late this afternoon," I said. "Back derailleur finally gave out."

"Doesn't surprise me," he said. "It wasn't working too well on our trip a couple of weeks ago."

"Yeah, the shifting's been pretty ragged. It'll be great to have it working smooth again."

"After school, do you want to come over and see my birthday loot?"

Zach had had his twelfth birthday a couple of weeks ago. Mary Ann, Sam, Ed, Stinky, and I had chipped in and given him a genuine, regulation-size pigskin football. It was a beaut and had set us back several allowances.

"Yeah," I said. "What else did you get?"

Zach grinned. "Some pretty good stuff. You'll see." He looked around at Mary Ann, Ed, and Stinky. "You guys want to come, too?"

"Sure," they said.

The bell rang and all the kids started walking in one huge crowd toward the school.

I felt a tap on my shoulder. I turned around and saw a girl with curly, short, dark hair.

She'd been in the group of squealers who had stared at Zach a minute earlier.

"You know that guy with the dark hair?" she said.

"Yeah," I said. I started to say, *I usually know the people I stand around with,* but I decided I might sound too smart, so I kept my mouth shut.

"What's his name?" she asked.

"Zach Walters," I said.

"Zach Walters? Oh, he's gorgeous!" she said, rolling her eyes. Then she turned to the girl standing next to her, the beautiful girl with all that blond hair. "Zach Walters!" she said breathlessly. The blonde glanced at me, nodded to her girl friend, and they moved on.

Zach, gorgeous? I almost laughed. Good old Zach. I shook my head and pressed toward the door. These girls didn't know anything about him, but they were acting weird because of the way he looked. I didn't get it.

There were lots of girls in the crowd surrounding me. Most of them looked like the Heather Parks–Jennifer Wilkes–Tiffany Brady squealer types. Somehow I had the feeling there weren't too many girls like Mary Ann and me in the crowd. I decided that during the day when we were in the orange and black groups,

I'd have to stick close to Ed and Stinky. Maybe I'd get to know some of the guys who'd played on the other metro teams last year.

I didn't know at the time, though, how tough that was going to be. I didn't know about the terrible thing that was already spreading through the school like some contagious disease. If I had, I might have headed home right then and refused ever to go to school again.

Because the kids in my class weren't the same kids I'd said good-bye to last spring at Washington Elementary.

They'd already started through The Change.

The first day of school is always hectic and crazy, but the first day of middle school was downright nuts.

Truman is big compared to Washington Elementary. It has three floors that all look the same: lockers line the halls in between classroom doors. I wondered how I'd remember what floor I was on, especially between classes when all the kids were rushing in every direction.

Kids were talking a lot in the hall as I made my way to homeroom.

"If you get Larson for social studies, don't

be late. I heard he yells at you in front of the whole class."

"I hope I don't have math before P.E. I can't go from the third floor way down to the gym in five minutes' passing time!"

"Don't let Mr. Brown hear you call him 'baldy.' He threw a kid out of class last year for that. He's real sensitive."

There was a lot to learn starting middle school. I hoped I could remember it all.

In homeroom everybody was assigned lockers. Our homeroom teacher, Ms. Embers, led us to our locker section along the wall on the second floor. We practiced opening them with the combination locks. The assignments were alphabetical, so I shared a locker with a girl named Ginger Flush. Turned out she was the squealer who'd asked me Zach's name before school.

I'm usually good at mechanical stuff, but my lock had me stumped. Of course, it didn't help that Ginger stood there flapping her mouth the whole time I was trying to figure it out.

"Do you know him?" she asked, pointing to a dark-haired kid tossing some of the stuff from his sports bag into a locker.

"Jeff Neidermeyer," I said. "He's a great

football player. Quarterback."

Ginger twisted strands of her curly, brown hair between two fingers. "He's gorgeous."

I stared at the paper with the three numbers on it. "I don't get it. I'm following the directions for this combination, but it still won't open."

I was getting pretty frustrated because most of the rest of the kids had their lockers open already. I felt sweat bloom on my forehead.

Ginger poked my arm. "Is that cutie in the blue shirt over there from your old school?"

I looked up. "Hunh-uh," I said. "He went to Jefferson. Mark McKey. He played third base for my metro baseball team."

"How about that hunk standing next to the water fountain?" she said.

"Matt Ryerson," I said impatiently. "Ginger, I'm trying to get this locker open, okay?"

"Gee," she said, "this is great. You must know every cute boy in this school."

"I played on the metro baseball and football teams," I said. "Just let me work on this lock now, okay?"

"So you're a jock!" she exclaimed. "What a super way to meet boys!"

I looked up at her. Ginger was some piece of work.

I tried the combination one more time.

She poked me in the back. "How about that boy with the reddish-blond hair over there?" she said.

I jerked around angrily and looked. "Yeah," I said. "That's my brother, Sam."

Her eyes practically bugged out of her head. "Your brother? Oh, wow, that's fantastic! He's a fox!"

"You've got to be kidding," I said.

"Hey," she said, "I wouldn't kid you about a cute boy. Put in a good word for me, okay?"

I stared at her. "I don't even *know* you."

"So?" she said. "We're locker partners!"

"Ginger," I said, "we were thrown together because of the first two letters of our last names. I've known you for two minutes."

"No, it's fate! Don't you see?" she said, beaming. "When we were born into our families—people whose names began with *FL*—we were destined to be put together. We're *supposed* to be friends. Isn't that great?"

What could I say to that? "Just great."

I went back to the combination.

Ms. Embers strolled by. She had big glasses and very long legs. She stood about twelve feet tall.

"Ms. Embers," I called out over the noise of

lockers slamming and kids talking. "I can't get this locker open."

She strode over to me in two gigantic steps. "Go ahead and try it again," she said.

I did and, like magic, it opened.

I felt my face heat up. Boy, did I feel dumb.

"See? No problem," said Ms. Embers. She strolled away.

The rest of the day wasn't much better. Most of the sixth-grade girls hung around in groups from their old schools, staring at and talking about kids from the other elementary schools. The boys hung around together, too, but they were quieter.

My classes, except for phys. ed., looked as if they were going to be pretty boring, even science, which is one of my better subjects. Language arts is my worst subject—all that reading and writing—but my teacher, Ms. Yeck (that's really her name; I wouldn't kid you) seemed kind of entertaining. Mary Ann said that her older sister told her that Ms. Yeck's name is Pearl, and the kids call her Squirrely Pearly, but not to her face. The word was that she was a fun teacher but you didn't learn a whole lot.

Anyway, Squirrely Pearly had each of us go up to the board and write our name. She said that you can learn a lot about people from the way they write their signatures. After she'd said that, all the girls tried to write in their most flowery handwriting. Heather Parks had the most rounded letters you ever saw, and Bonnie Wilson dotted her *i*'s with little hearts. I almost laughed out loud at that.

The guys wrote in messy scrawls on purpose. Even Adam Matthews, whose handwriting usually looks like an electric typewriter, scratched his name in an unreadable scribble. I printed, as usual—I hate writing in cursive—and, as usual, you could read it, but you had to look close.

Ed Mechtensteimer, who sat two seats away from me, grinned as I walked back to my seat and gave me a thumbs-up sign. "Says a lot about your character," he said.

"Oh, yeah? What does it say?" I asked him.

"That you're almost as smart as I am."

I grinned and rolled my eyes. "You wish, Mechtenstupid."

Nathan Morgan, sitting between us, cracked up at that. "If I have to look at someone's paper during a test," he said, "I'm looking at Lizard's."

"I heard that, Nathan," Squirrely Pearly said. "We move our desks around the room during a test. You'll be right next to me."

Everybody laughed, even Nathan, who got a red face.

It was kind of hard to sit there in class and breathe normally. Chris Mulray, a fun girl who had started a great food fight in the cafeteria last year, was sitting next to me. Chris was wearing even more perfume than my aunt Amanda, and you can tell that my aunt's been in a room a day after she's gone home.

Anyway, when Chris got up and walked to the blackboard, she stirred up the air as she walked by, and I nearly passed out. I looked at Ed, grabbed my throat, and stuck out my tongue. He and Nathan grinned and started coughing loudly.

I looked at the raised window next to the pencil sharpener and put up my hand.

"Yes, Elizabeth?" said Squirrely Pearly.

Ed stopped coughing, looked at me and snickered.

"Can I sharpen my pencil?" I asked.

"You won't be needing your pencil today," Squirrely said.

"Then can I stick my head out the window? I need some fresh air."

Some of the kids laughed, and Chris turned around from the blackboard. She'd just written *Christine* in big, loopy letters.

Squirrel Pearly tried not to smile. "Okay, but just for a minute."

I walked to the window and took a deep breath of air.

Ed put up his hand. "Me, too?"

"How about a gas mask?" Tom Luther said from across the room.

Everybody cracked up except Chris, who glared at me and hurried back to her chair.

"*Christine?*" said Nathan, reading her name off the board. "You're Christine this year?"

"Yeah," Chris snapped. "You have a problem with that, Nathan?"

I looked at Chris. Last year she'd aimed a spoonful of mashed potatoes halfway across the cafeteria and scored a direct hit on Tiffany Brady. Now she was almost acting like Tiffany. Why would Chris start dowsing herself with perfume and want to be called *Christine?* Normally, she would've decked Nathan Morgan for teasing her. And what was this Nathan stuff? Last year he was Morgan. She sure had changed over the summer.

"Ready for lunch?" Ed asked me after class.

"Yeah," I said. "You too?"

"Yeah. Man, I'm hungry!"

I grinned at him. "You're always hungry, Mechtensteimer."

22

We walked down the crowded hall, getting jostled on all sides. A bright-red poster welcoming everyone back to school was on the wall near the entrance to the cafeteria. Next to it was another poster announcing a Welcome to Truman Middle School dance for sixth graders. It seemed as if there were posters everywhere. I'd already seen them advertising the chess club, the math club, and tryouts for the fall play.

"Hey, Lizard!" Zach was standing with Stinky at the cafeteria door. He grinned at me. "You guys eat now?"

"Yeah."

"Great."

"At least we have lunch together," I said.

We left our books on a table in the middle of the room and got in line behind Mike Herman and Andy Walinsky.

"So who's going to win the World Series?" Mike said.

"Atlanta," Andy said.

"The Cardinals," said Stinky.

"It doesn't matter who's going to win the World Series," I said. "What's important is who the best team is."

"Uh-oh," Ed said. "Don't get Lizard started on baseball. She's obsessed with the Cubs."

I ignored him. "The Chicago Cubs aren't getting to the World Series, but they're still the best all-around team in the country."

Stinky snorted. "Yeah, right! If the Cubs are so good, why haven't they been in the top of their division for the last hundred years? If a team is good, they'll get to the World Series at some point."

"You're full of it, Stinky," I said. "Look at their long-term record. Look at Mark Grace. Look at Ryne Sandberg."

"Yeah," Zach said. "The World Series doesn't take underdog victories into account, either. Lizard's right. You've got to look at the long-term record of the team."

The line moved along to the ticket desk. "You can get a week's supply of lunch tickets for five dollars," said the woman in the white uniform. She looked tired and sounded as if she'd said that line a thousand times today. "Otherwise, today's lunch is a dollar twenty-five."

I handed her money for one lunch.

"What are we eating today?" I asked her.

"Sloppy joes," she said.

"My brother told me the only good food here is the pizza," Stinky said.

The woman scowled at him.

I took a yellow tray and walked down the line while the women behind the counter served up my food. They handed me the plate at the end of the line, and I went back to our lunch table.

"The Yankees are my team," Ed said. "Don Mattingly's the best first baseman in the country."

I turned to him. "No way. Mark Grace is more consistent. On top of that, the Cubs have—no question—the best second baseman in the history of baseball."

"Yeah," Zach said. "Sandberg must've won a dozen Gold Glove awards."

"Oh, yeah, right, a dozen," Stinky said, his mouth full of hamburger.

I scooped up a spoonful of apple salad and glanced over at the next table. Ginger Flush sat with the beautiful blonde girl who'd stared at Zach before school. Some other squealers were there, too. They were looking at us and whispering. Ginger's face lit up like fireworks in a summer sky when she saw me looking at her, and she waved. I nodded to her.

I turned back to Zach. He was talking about the fishing trip he'd taken last week with his dad to the boundary waters in northeastern Minnesota.

"The mosquitoes grow as big as humming-birds up there," he was saying. "You lie in your tent at night and you can hear millions of them buzzing all around you in the woods."

"Big as hummingbirds?" Stinky sneered.

"Really," Zach said. "A man stripped naked would be drained of all his blood in two hours."

"I bet." Stinky was still skeptical.

"From the mosquitoes?" Ed said. "No way."

All the guys were listening with their mouths open. "Zach's right," I said. "My family went camping once in Canada. We rubbed insect repellent all over us, even under our clothes, but that didn't stop the mosquitoes. They bit us right through our clothes. We had welts all over us the size of quarters."

"Oh, man, that's disgusting," Mike said. Now they were all looking at me.

"Sam and I tried sleeping in the car, but the mosquitoes came through the vents to get us."

The guys shivered at the thought.

I felt a tap on my shoulder.

"Oh, Liz," said Ginger Flush, who had appeared suddenly at my side. "This is my friend, Lisa St. George." She turned to the girl standing next to her. "Lisa, this is Liz Flanagan, my *locker partner.*" She said those last two words as if I were a celebrity or something.

"It's Lizard," I said. "Not Liz."

Ginger giggled. "Whatever," she said, smiling. "'A rose by any other name would smell as sweet!' That's Shakespeare." No one said anything, but Lisa looked at her and rolled her eyes. "Well, I just wanted you two to meet."

Lisa was a living Barbie doll. Her hair was blond and flowing, and her eyes were big and swimming-pool blue. Even her teeth were straight and white. It was irritating just looking at her.

There were three other girls with Ginger, but she didn't bother to introduce them. They stood there with little smiles on their faces, looking around at the guys sitting at the table. One girl was chomping on a big wad of gum. She snapped it, and it sounded like a pistol shot.

Out of the corner of my eye I saw three figures approach. I turned just in time to see one of the girls stumble into Lisa, nearly knocking her over.

Lisa glared at the girl and said under her breath, "Get out of my sight, you geek." Only Ginger and I—and the girl she'd said it to— heard her.

The girl's face turned red; she looked both angry and embarrassed.

"Come on, Shannon," said one of her friends.

Shannon glowered at Lisa, then hurried off with the two girls.

Ginger looked at me. "Those girls really get on Lisa's nerves," she whispered. "Especially Shannon."

"How come?"

She shrugged. "Probably just because they exist. All three—Shannon, Angie, and Cheryl—are from our old school. Shannon used to be Lisa's best friend, but Lisa's really cool now and doesn't like Shannon anymore."

I looked over to see Lisa staring at Zach across the table. Her mouth was partly open in a tiny smile.

I looked over at Zach. He glanced self-consciously over at Lisa, then down at his sloppy joe.

The other guys at the table were acting as weird as Zach, shifting back and forth in their seats as if they had ants in their pants.

Ginger went on talking. "Liz, after school—"

"Lizard," I said.

"Oh, yeah. Anyway, after school we're all going to go to the mall. Stylers is having a humongous back-to-school sale. You want to come with us?"

I'd never been in Stylers, but I'd heard the girls in my class talk about it. It sells expensive clothes—the kind you see on models on TV. I prefer the Gap and the sportswear department at Sears, myself.

"No," I said. "Thanks, but I'm going over to Zach's house after school." I heard the girls, all together, take in a quick breath. "He's going to show me the stuff he got for his birthday."

"Ohhh," said Lisa. She beamed a megawatt smile at Zach. "You just had a birthday?"

Zach's ears turned pink and he said, "Yeah," so softly I could hardly hear him. Stinky snorted and elbowed him in the ribs. Zach elbowed him back and glanced all around him, everywhere but at the girls.

"You turned twelve, Zach?" Lisa asked.

"Yeah," Zach said.

"You're *older* than we are!" Ginger said. "I don't have my birthday until January. I'm a Capricorn."

No one commented on that bit of trivia, but the guys all looked at one another and grinned more idiotically than before.

"My birthday is in March," Lisa offered.

"She's an Aries," Ginger added.

No one said anything. I couldn't think of anything to say either, so I nodded and said, "Great."

"Well, we'll see you guys later," Ginger said. "Don't worry about not coming with us, Liz—ard. We'll get together later."

"I'm not worried," I said. The girls left. I turned to the guys. "Why would she think I'd be worried?"

They ignored my question. Ed turned to Zach and punched him on the arm. "You see Lisa gawking at you, Walters? I think she's *in love!*"

"Shut up, Mechtensteimer!" Zach's ears were bright red by now, and the rest of the face was catching up.

"She's beautiful, Walters," Stinky teased. "I think you should *go for it!*"

"Hey, did you see the poster for the dance?" Ed said. "It's a Welcome to Truman Middle School dance for sixth graders next Friday after school. You could take Lisa."

"You could dance with her," Stinky said. "Real close. Maybe even kiss her!"

"What are you guys talking about?" I said, suddenly irritable. "Zach isn't interested in her!"

"I think he is," Ed said, grinning. "You see how red his face is?"

Andy leaned over and batted his eyelashes and made loud kissing noises.

Ed laughed. "Let's call Lisa back and tell her." He stood up, looking for Lisa.

Zach lunged at Ed and knocked him on the floor. He scrambled over and put a headlock on him. "Yeah?" Zach said. "Well, you can stick it in your ear, Mechtensteimer!"

"Geez, let go, will you?" Ed said. His face was turning purple from lack of air.

Mr. Sanders, the lunchroom supervisor (you can translate that as *warden*), saw Zach and Ed on the floor and charged toward them. Zach saw him coming and let go of Ed.

"No more of that!" Mr. Sanders said, pointing at Zach.

"I was only kidding, Walters," Ed said, rubbing his neck. Then he grinned. "But I still think you should go for it."

"You guys weren't any better than Zach was in front of those girls!" I said to Ed and Stinky and Mike and Andy. "You squirmed around, grinning like idiots the whole time they were standing here!"

"They were starin' right at us!" Stinky said.

"So what?" I said. "Haven't you ever seen *girls* before?"

There was a little silence before Ed said with awe, "Not like them."

I didn't like his tone of voice.

I looked over at Zach, who was staring into space wearing a dumb expression.

What's the matter with these bozos? I thought. They were all acting subhuman—like strangers.

I didn't know it yet, but that's exactly what they were turning into.

My closest friends were starting through The Change.

3

"I gotta talk to you!"

Even over the noise of banging lockers in the hall, I heard Ginger yell. It was the end of the day and everybody was dumping their school stuff and heading for home.

Ginger rushed up, stopped right in front of me, and pushed her face into mine. "I gotta talk to you!" she said again. I noticed that she still had a little apple salad from lunch stuck in her braces. I backed up a step.

"What about?" I asked her.

"How did you do it?" she asked breathlessly.

"Do what?"

"How did you get yourself invited to Zach Walters's house?" Ginger's eyes bored into mine.

I took another step back. "I didn't do anything to get myself invited," I said. "He just asked me to come over."

Ginger collapsed against the locker next to ours.

"He's so gorgeous, I just can't believe it," she said.

I was about to say, "So what?" but she didn't stop jabbering long enough to give me the chance.

"You're going to his house right now?"

"Yeah—" I said.

"You're so lucky to be his girlfriend," Ginger said.

"I'm not his girlfriend. I mean, I'm a girl and I'm his friend, but—"

"You're not his girlfriend?"

"No," I said. "Zach's my pal. We've been friends since practically forever."

"Your *pal*?" Ginger looked at me as if she couldn't believe it. "You mean to tell me you're just friends?"

"Yeah."

She stared at me for a long moment as if she were trying to understand something that was

34

too complicated for her. Finally she started to smile. "Gee, that's great!"

"What?" I said.

"Lisa will be so happy! She's been depressed all afternoon thinking that you're Zach's girlfriend."

That was the dumbest thing I'd ever heard, but I let it pass.

"Okay," I said. "See you tomorrow."

"I can't wait to find her and tell her the good news!"

"'Bye," I said.

She waved and hurried off down the hall. I watched her go. It was going to be a long year having Ginger as a locker partner.

I found Mary Ann waiting just outside.

"I'm going home to change," she said. "Then I'll meet you guys at Zach's house."

"Kind of hot in the old panty hose?" I couldn't resist saying it, but I tried not to smile too much.

"It wasn't too bad," she said. I knew she was lying because she didn't look at me.

We walked together down the sidewalk. She would be turning off in a few blocks to go to her house.

"So how were your classes?" I asked her.

"Okay," she said. "I think science and

language arts will be good. I like the teachers, and the kids seem nice. How about yours?"

"Boring," I said. "I don't have P.E. till tomorrow, but I'm sure that'll be fun."

"Did you meet anyone new who seems nice?"

"Not really," I said. "I mostly hung out with Ed and Stinky. They were in most of my classes. Zach and Andy and Mike had lunch with us. Too bad you missed it."

"I guess I kind of want to branch out this year," she said.

Branching out made me think of squirrels.

"I've got Squirrely Pearly for language arts," I said. "I've heard she doesn't make you write very much."

"Oh," Mary Ann said. "I've got Mrs. Peddycoart. She says we'll be writing poetry in class."

"I like poetry," I said. "Especially if it's funny. Like 'There was an old lady from Lynn, who—'"

"That's a limerick," she said.

"Yeah," I said. "Don't you want to hear it?"

"Sure."

"There was an old lady from Lynn,
Who was so exceedingly thin

That when she assayed
To drink lemonade,
She slipped through the straw and fell in."

"That's a good one," Mary Ann said. "But I think Mrs. Peddycoart meant regular poetry. Some of it doesn't even rhyme."

"Why would anyone write a poem that doesn't rhyme?"

"I don't know," Mary Ann said. "I think poetry that doesn't rhyme is supposed to be more sophisticated or something. Mrs. Peddycoart said we'll be doing more advanced things than we did in elementary school."

"Oh."

We'd arrived at the corner where Mary Ann was going to turn off.

"I'll see you at Zach's," she said.

"Right," I said. "See you."

Zach's house wasn't far, about three blocks. I decided to time myself and see how long it took me to run there.

I stretched a bit to warm up. Then I set the timer on my watch, picked a crack on the sidewalk as my starting line, and crouched.

"Ready, set, *go!*" I said, and took off.

The guys were sitting on Zach's front porch, their bicycles scattered around the yard.

"Here she comes," Sam called out.

I really pulled out all the stops then, and tore past the porch in a final burst of speed.

"You run from school?" Sam asked.

I breathed hard and walked with my arms resting on the top of my head, cooling down.

"No," I said. "From the corner of Hutcheson and River."

"What was your time?" Zach asked.

I checked my watch. "One forty-two," I said.

"Not too bad," Sam said.

"What do you mean, not too bad?" I said. "That was a great time!"

"I could do it faster," Ed said.

Stinky snorted. Zach and Sam grinned.

I turned to Ed. "No way, Mechtenslowpoke. I've always been able to beat you. By miles!"

"Maybe not anymore, though," he said, grinning. "Girls are supposed to slow down and guys speed up at about twelve."

"What? That's the dumbest thing I've ever heard!"

"It's a well-known fact," Ed said. He looked at Sam, then Zach and Stinky. "Aren't I right?"

Sam smirked. "Yeah."

"No way! That's ridiculous!"

"That's the way it is," Ed said, "so get used to it."

"Okay, smart guy," I said, turning to Ed. "We'll race later. And I'll *still* beat you."

"You're on."

"Where's Mary Ann?" Zach asked as we went inside.

"Home changing. She'll be here pretty soon."

Zach's dog, Klondike, leaped up and danced all over the floor, he was so happy to see us. Klondike is a Lab mix and has a gentle, happy nature. He's so big, though, he can knock you over while he's saying hello.

Zach has a great room. The ceiling is covered with little plastic moons and stars that glow in the dark. The walls are covered with posters of his—and my—favorite ballplayers (Ryne Sandberg, of course, and Mark Grace) and a Chicago Cubs team picture.

A shelf over his desk is lined with all the trophies he's won. Last year the Raiders, our flag football team, voted him MVP, and he shared MVP honors with me on our baseball team, the Hawks. Then there were trophies for fishing competitions in Minnesota.

Today his floor was covered with dirty

clothes he hadn't had time to put in the hamper.

I flopped on the bed and Klondike climbed on top of me. He huffed his dog breath into my face, but I didn't mind. I'd rather have Klondike in my face any day than Ginger Flush.

"Okay, Walters," I said, scratching Klondike's neck, "let's see your loot."

Zach grinned and went to his closet. He pulled out his tackle box, shoved aside some baseball cards on his desk, and set it down.

I pushed Klondike aside and joined the guys who crowded around his desk.

"A wet fly lure," Zach said, taking it carefully out of this box.

It had glossy brown and reddish feathers that would drag through the water on his hook and attract fish by the dozens.

"The trout and bass'll fight to get a chance at it," I said enviously.

A voice from downstairs called out. "Hi, everybody!"

"Hi, Mary Ann!" Zach yelled. "We're in my room."

In a few seconds, Mary Ann appeared at the door. She was wearing her old blue cotton shorts and a T-shirt that said "Planet Hollywood—New York."

"Mary Ann!" I said. "They let you go!"

"What do you mean?"

"Your kidnappers. They sent someone in your place this morning," I said. "A girl showed up at school pretending to be you. Her disguise was good, but one thing gave her away. She was wearing panty hose."

Mary Ann shrugged. "Yeah. I fought them off. I overcame all five of them with my incredible strength."

Zach grinned. "Hey, I noticed the skirt today, Mary Ann. You looked good."

"Thanks."

Zach showed us some more of his birthday stuff: a really great baseball computer game, a book about Heisman winners, and a knife for cleaning fish.

"And then the usual clothes," Zach said, shrugging.

No one wanted to see them, so we went outside.

"You guys want to play a game of football?" I asked. "Zach's team against mine."

"We'll break in Zach's new ball," Sam said.

"Okay, Klondike," Zach said. "You'll have

to sit next to the fence." He pushed Klondike into a sitting position. "Stay."

Klondike gazed up at Zach, his tongue hanging out the side of his mouth. He looked disappointed.

It was a good game. Mary Ann, Sam, and I were against Zach, Ed, and Stinky. We won the toss, and I said we'd receive. The end zones were four bushes, two at either end of the yard.

Zach kicked off and Mary Ann received the ball.

She dodged both Ed and Stinky, but Zach got by Sam and tagged her halfway to the bush. Klondike whined and wagged his tail.

"Hey, Zach, Klondike wants to play," I said.

"He could probably show us a few pointers," Zach said. "He's a big Miami fan—watches every game."

On the next play, Zach handed off the ball to Ed, who tried to run it up the middle. I easily tagged him. Sam gave me a high five. Klondike stood up and barked.

"Easy, boy. Stay," Zach said, patting him on the head.

On the next play, Sam snapped the ball and motioned for me to move farther down the yard. I trotted backward with Zach covering me. I was geared up for this; I love the chance to run for a touchdown.

Sam threw a perfect spiral. The ball landed right in my fingertips. Zach tried to tag me, but I darted out of his way and ran past the bushes for a touchdown.

"All right!" I danced around the bushes with my arms in the air. Sam and Mary Ann were cheering, too.

Out of nowhere, Klondike leaped up and knocked me to the ground, barking and licking my face.

"Klondike, get off!" I yelled, laughing. Finally, I pushed him back and stood up.

"Klondike can't help it," Zach said, grinning. "He wants to be a linebacker."

We got drinks of water at the outdoor spigot near the back door.

"Hey, Lizard, your arm's bleeding," Mary Ann said.

I hadn't known I'd scratched myself till she pointed to the blood trickling down my elbow.

"You better clean that up," Zach said.

He and I went inside and into the kitchen. He pulled a bandage out of a drawer and handed it to me. I washed the cut and put the bandage over it.

"Hey, Lizard. Want one?"

Zach opened the top of the cookie jar. I

could smell the peanut butter three feet away.

"So how was your first day of school?" I asked him.

He shrugged and held out the jar. "Fine. How about yours?"

"Okay," I said. "I wish you and Sam and Mary Ann were in the orange group." I took a cookie.

"Me, too." Zach grabbed a cookie and set the jar on the kitchen table.

"I can't believe some of the girls in my classes," I said. "Like that Ginger Flush."

"The girl who came over during lunch?"

I made a face. "What an airhead. And those girls who squeal all the time—"

"Mmm."

"Listen to this," I said, pushing a strand of hair back from my face. "Ginger came up to me after school and said that girl, Lisa St. George—you know, the one with the big hair— was all broken up because she thought I was your girlfriend!" I laughed.

Zach's eyes got a little bigger and he swallowed the cookie in his mouth. "Really?"

"Yeah," I said. "She wants to be your girlfriend, and she's been sad because she thinks you're already taken!"

44

"What did you tell Ginger?"

I shrugged. "I told her we're best friends, of course. Boy, those girls are so dumb!"

Zach pulled out another cookie but didn't put it in his mouth. He fingered the edge of the cookie jar.

"What do you know about that Lisa—what's her name?"

I had the weird feeling that he really did remember.

"St. George."

"Oh, yeah," he said, nodding. He was still running his finger around the jar. "So—what do you know about her?"

"Nothing. She doesn't seem very friendly, though."

He looked out the window and didn't say anything.

"Come on," I said. Just thinking about Lisa and those girls ticked me off. "Let's take some cookies out to the guys."

He continued to stare out the window.

"Hey, Earth to Walters!"

He jerked his head to look at me.

"You coming?"

"Sure," he said.

We went outside and played some more,

but it wasn't as much fun. Zach's head wasn't in the game anymore. He missed passes and didn't tag me twice when he should have.

I watched him while we played football and hoped that maybe he was just coming down with a cold or something. Something that would pass so he'd be the good old Zach I've always known.

But it wasn't going to pass. It was going to get a lot worse.

4

"Have you ever heard that girls are supposed to slow down at twelve?" I asked Mary Ann on the way home. "And that boys are supposed to get better in athletics?"

"Well, most men's bodies are built to be stronger," she said. "But I've heard that women are beginning to catch up in speed. You don't have anything to worry about. You beat the heck out of Ed just now."

"Yeah."

But I didn't want to think that he might—someday—be able to beat me.

We reached the next corner. "You want to stop by the creek before we go home?" I said.

"Sure."

We turned left, and halfway down the block, we veered off into the woods.

I've loved the woods ever since I was a little kid. They surround a wide, shallow ravine with a creek running along the bottom. The creek is full of minnows, newts, and about a million frogs.

Compared to the sun-heated furnace of the sidewalk, the woods felt cool and moist. We ran over the rim of the ravine and down the side. At the bottom we stopped and sat on a log at the edge of the creek.

"I'm thinking of getting my hair cut," Mary Ann said.

"Why?"

"It's getting too long," she said, twisting a strand of her long, brown hair around her finger. "It's in the way."

I shrugged. "Just tie it back with a rubber band the way you do when we play ball."

Another long moment of silence went by.

"I think I'll get it cut," she said.

"Okay. You can always grow it back if you don't like it."

"That's what I was thinking."

I took off my shoes, sat on the bank of the creek, and put my feet in the cool water.

"Feels good," I said. "Take your shoes off."

She joined me on the bank, slipped off her shoes, and dipped her feet in the water.

"Did you see the posters around school about the dance next Friday?" she asked.

"Yeah."

"You want to go?"

"No," I said.

"It might be fun," Mary Ann said. "My sister went to some of the dances at Truman and really liked them."

"Well, no offense," I said, "but your sister's different from us."

"What do you mean?"

"I mean, she's more like the other girls in our class."

Mary Ann frowned. "In what way?"

"You know," I said. "She wears skirts and makeup."

"What does that have to do with going to a school dance?" Mary Ann's voice was higher than usual.

"Nothing," I said. "I just mean that Karen is more of a . . ." I paused.

"A what?"

"You know. A girly-girl."

"You make that sound like a bad thing. There's nothing wrong with my sister!"

"I didn't mean there's anything wrong with her," I said. "But just because Karen liked the dances doesn't mean we'll like them."

"I bet I'll like this dance," Mary Ann said. "And I'm planning to go."

"What's so great about a dance?" I said.

"Dancing, dummy!"

"But you've never danced before," I said. "You don't even know how."

"I don't have to know how," she said. "You just move to the music. I've watched my sister and her friends."

I slapped my feet on the surface of the water.

"Well, I'm not going to waste my time."

"Suit yourself." She got up and put on her shoes.

"Where are you going?"

"Home," she said. "I've got some problems to do for math tomorrow."

"Okay," I said. I knew Mary Ann was ticked off at me, and I didn't like the feeling that gave me in my stomach. Why would she want to go to a stupid school dance? Anything would be more fun than that!

"I have to get my bike anyway," I said. "It's supposed to be ready now."

"Then we'll be riding to school tomorrow?" Mary Ann said.

"Yeah," I said. "Meet you at the bridge over the ravine?"

"At seven thirty," she said.

"Right," I said. "I'm bringing my football, so no skirts."

Mary Ann's jaw got tight. "Who died and made *you* boss?"

I didn't say anything.

She turned away. "I'm going home now. See you tomorrow."

"See you."

Without waiting for me, she climbed up the side of the ravine and disappeared over the ridge.

It hadn't been one of my better days. A lot of crummy things had happened in the last nine hours: I'd started back to prison, my friends were suddenly acting like weird strangers, and now Mary Ann was mad at me.

So far, middle school was the pits.

5

At last, on the second day of school, we had the class I'd been waiting for: P.E. I love phys. ed. I mean, you get to spend the whole period playing baseball or flag football or some other game, and then you get a good grade for it. Who could ask for a better class?

Ms. Puff, our P.E. teacher, took roll while we sat on the floor in the gym. Ms. Puff wore white shorts and a pink shirt. We girls were dressed in whatever we'd worn to school that day. We'd brought the T-shirts and shorts that we'd wear during gym class.

The floor smelled of wax just like the gym floor at Washington Elementary always did during the first few weeks of school. It was polished, too, and shone so bright that Ms. Puff's image was reflected off the shiny surface.

Her reflection didn't look a whole lot like her, though. It didn't show how tall she was, and it didn't show all the nose hairs sticking out of her nostrils or the darkness at the roots of her potato chip–colored hair.

"Now, girls," she called out after she'd taken roll, "I'm going to take you downstairs to the locker room. You'll each be assigned a locker and a combination lock."

Just what I need, I thought, another lock. At least I didn't have to share my locker with anyone.

"Go ahead, girls, and change into your gym clothes," Ms. Puff said. "We're playing softball with the boys."

"It would be cool to be in Zach's class," Lisa said to Ginger and Heather. "I'd like to see him play."

"Yeah," Ginger said, turning to me with a grin. "I bet he looks sexy in his gym shorts. Bet Sam does, too."

Heather laughed and Lisa smiled in that cool way of hers. What an ice princess.

"Well, I'm glad you're interested in what really matters," I said sarcastically.

"You bet!" Ginger said. "Is there anything that matters more about a guy than his bod?"

Heather squealed. She sounded like one of the little pigs on my uncle's farm.

We all started changing into our gym clothes. Boy, was I surprised. They all wore bras! There were only three girls besides me who weren't wearing one. I didn't want to stare, so I just glanced around every couple of seconds or so. Some of the girls needed bras, some of them didn't. Some were sort of on the borderline.

If you must know, I was one of the borderline cases, leaning toward not needing one, which was fine with me.

Lisa needed a bra and wore one.

I didn't think any girls had worn bras last year. But then I couldn't be sure. What had happened over the summer? It was weird how everyone seemed to be turning into different people.

We waited at the door in a clump to go outside. That is, all but Lisa and Ginger. They stood in their gym clothes (that looked brand-new, for crying out loud) in front of the mirrors, combing their hair.

Shannon, the girl who'd bumped into Lisa at lunch on the first day, stood with her friends,

Angie and Cheryl, near Heather and me. They watched Lisa as she pulled the comb through her thick wavy hair.

Lisa glanced over and saw them looking at her. "What are you three geeks staring at?"

"Nothing," Shannon said.

She turned her back to Lisa and murmured to her friends, "What an egomaniac." They giggled.

Heather walked over to Lisa and whispered in her ear. Lisa coolly turned and gazed at the three girls. "If I were as ugly as you three, I wouldn't want to see myself in the mirror."

An embarrassed giggle went through the crowd of girls.

Shannon and her friends turned bright red with anger and embarrassment. Shannon's eyes narrowed and she whispered something to them. They nodded and glared at Lisa.

"Why are you guys combing your hair now?" Heather asked, looking at Lisa's reflection over her shoulder. "It'll just get messy again outside."

"So?" Ginger said. "The boys are out there, remember?"

"Oh, yeah!" Heather said, rushing to her school bag.

Several other girls hurried to their bags to

grab their combs and brushes. One of them, Sara Pulliam, even pulled out a tiny container of perfume and sprayed it on her neck.

"In case I sweat," she said to Heather. "This'll cover up the smell."

I looked at some girls standing next to me and rolled my eyes, but no one said anything.

"We don't have time for that, girls," Ms. Puff called out. "Let's go."

Ms. Puff led us outside through the locker-room door, and we climbed the small hill to the softball diamond.

I walked behind Shannon, Angie, and Cheryl. They were talking, and I heard Shannon say, "She'll gets hers someday."

I didn't blame her for being mad.

When we got to the top of the hill, the guys were already there. Stinky and Ed stepped out of the crowd of guys and walked over to me.

"What took you so long?" Stinky complained. "We've been waiting for twenty minutes."

"Five minutes, Stinky," Ed corrected him.

"You can't believe what these girls do to get ready to play softball," I said.

Stinky's and Ed's eyes got big. They glanced at each other and back at me. "What do they do?" they said together.

56

"You don't want to know," I said.

The boys' gym teacher, Mr. Grodin, was a big guy with hairy legs. He called out, "Ed Mechtensteimer, you'll be captain of your team."

"And Jennifer Peterson," called out Ms. Puff, "you will be captain of your team."

Mr. Grodin pulled a coin out of his pocket. "What'll it be, Mechtensteimer?" He tossed the coin in the air.

"Heads," Ed said.

Mr. Grodin caught the coin and slapped it onto his other hand. "Heads it is," he said. "You get first choice."

"All right!" Ed said. He turned and surveyed the crowd of kids. He grinned at me. "Lizard."

Some of the girls started to murmur as if they were surprised.

I grinned at Ed and walked over to him. I looked around at all the kids in the class and figured I was probably the best player there. No brag, just fact.

Jennifer picked Tom Luther next. That was a good move; Tom had a .600 batting average in the metro league. Ed picked Stinky next, then he and Jennifer took turns till all the kids were on one team or another. Ginger and Lisa were picked last. In a way I felt sorry for them. It must have been really embarrassing to stand there knowing that no one wanted you.

Then we started playing ball, and I stopped feeling sorry. They were the worst players I'd ever seen! Lisa was on our team, and Ginger was on Jennifer's. When it was our turn in the field, Ed put Lisa in center field. I was pitching, Ed was on third base, and Stinky was shortstop. Tom Luther came up to bat.

"Watch him, he's tough," I heard Ed say to Nathan Morgan, who was playing first base.

I wasn't about to pitch an easy one to Luther. He was a pro. I wound up and threw my curve. Tom swung and missed. Strike one. I nodded. Next I pitched a fastball. This time he managed to connect and popped the ball up to center field. It would be an easy out. I looked over to see who would catch it.

Lisa was standing right under the ball. Her arms were folded; she looked as if she were daydreaming.

"Lisa!" I screamed. "Get the ball!"

Lisa shaded her eyes with her hand.

"What?"

"The *ball*!"

Plop. It landed right at her feet.

Lisa looked at the ball, then up at me. She

strolled over to the ball and picked it up.

"Throw it here!" Ed yelled.

She threw it in his direction, but it only went a few feet and fell to the ground. She shrugged, threw her long hair over one shoulder, and started talking to Heather.

By that time, Luther had his run.

Time to get serious, I thought. I got the next three batters out with my fastball.

"Good going, Lizard!" Stinky called out.

Now it was our turn at bat. I was up first.

Josh Meachum was pitching.

"Sock it out of the park, Lizard!" Ed yelled. "Show 'em what you've got!"

I knew Josh had a good fastball. I waited to see what he'd dish up for me.

It was his curve. I swung and hit it high into right field. That was Ginger's position. "Ooo, ooo," she said, running for the ball. "I got it, I got it, I got it!" The ball hit her hands and bounced to the ground. She scooped it up and threw it to first base, but I was already there.

"Close," she said, "but no cigar."

I made it around the bases on the next three pitches. I think Meachum was giving some easy pitches to the girls on our team. He's a nice guy.

Not nice enough, though. After a few

innings we were ahead, 9 to 3, so he struck out three of the next five hitters. We were back in the field.

The next four batters, all guys on the metro teams, got runs. The score was 9 to 7. They were catching up.

I really wanted to win my first middle-school game, even if was just in gym class. Maybe it was superstition, but I wanted to start out the school year on the right foot.

Ginger was up next.

"Be nice," she said to me. "Remember, we're locker partners."

I wound up and threw her my curveball. I didn't feel like being nice.

She swung hard and missed. She grabbed her nose, laughing, and spun around in a circle. "I thought you were going to be *nice*," she said.

She looked so embarrassed, I felt sort of sorry for her. Next time, I threw her a cream puff, but she fanned again. She even missed the third easy pitch. She was beyond help.

Her team got two runs. Then I struck out two more hitters.

The score was 9 to 9, and we were up at bat.

We scored three runs before the inning was over.

I looked at my watch. I knew we'd had our last run. Now we just had to keep Jennifer's team from getting runs and tying us or winning the game.

I struck out the first batter. The next four batters up were metro players, and they were good. The first got a hit, the second doubled, then the third batter singled. Those metro guys were having a good day.

The score was 12 to 9 and the bases were loaded. There was only a minute or so of playing time left, and everyone knew this play might end the game in a tie.

Tom Luther was up at bat. I threw him my curve, but he was ready for it. He knocked a high fly ball out to center field.

"Walinsky!" I screamed. "Get it!"

But he wasn't close enough. I knew he couldn't run that fast.

"Lisa!" I screamed.

She was talking to Heather but looked up. She didn't move, but the ball flew right to her as if it were a radar-controlled missile.

Lisa raised her arms a bit to shield her face. *Wham!* The ball landed right in her hands.

No one was more surprised than Lisa.

While the kids cheered, she stood there with huge eyes and stared back at them. Then she smiled and held her fists high in the air and whooped.

I was glad she'd caught the ball for our team, but I had to marvel at what the odds must have been for that to happen. Maybe a thousand to one. Or a million.

"Let's go!" shouted Mr. Grodin. "Mechtensteimer's team wins!"

We headed back to the school building. Ed ran past Lisa and yelled, "Good going, Lisa! Great play!"

She smiled and nodded as if she deserved the compliment and held her fists in the air again.

I wasn't about to congratulate her. Her "great play" was a fluke. Out of thirty minutes of play time, she'd stood around for twenty-nine minutes and fifty-five seconds, then held up her hands and won the game.

I couldn't stand it.

At the school building the boys and girls separated. "Did you see the posters for the sixth-grade dance?" Sara said to Jennifer as we tromped into the locker room.

"Yeah," she said. "Next Friday night, right?"

The mob of girls coming into the locker

room slowed and stopped in a big clump. I was stuck in the middle.

"Yeah. Are you planning to go?" Sara said. "*Everyone* will be there."

Lisa nodded to Ginger and smiled.

"I bet Zach'll be there," Ginger said. She turned and saw me staring at them. "Won't he, Lizard?"

"I don't know," I said. I couldn't imagine Zach going to a dumb school dance, but then he'd been acting weird lately, so I didn't know for sure.

I gently pushed my way out of the clump and walked to my locker. My stomach had suddenly gotten sour.

"So you think Ed will tell Zach about my great catch and how I won the game?"

I turned around to see Lisa gazing at me.

"You asking me?"

"Of course I'm asking you. You think Ed'll tell him?"

I shrugged. "Maybe."

"I bet Ed tells him about your winning the game," Ginger said, coming up behind Lisa. "He was impressed. *Major* impressed."

"Girls!" Ms. Puff hollered. She stood next to the shower room holding a clipboard.

63

"Come over here, will you?"

We walked over to her. "All of you are required to take showers after class. I'll check you off as you walk by. If you're having your period, you don't have to shower."

The locker room was suddenly silent as a tomb. I glanced away from Ms. Puff.

She had just come right out and said it. *If you're having your period—*

I looked at the faces around me. Everybody was looking at everybody else. I saw a lot of embarrassed smiles.

I wouldn't start my period for a long time. I was sure of it. Didn't that happen to girls much older? I didn't even want to think about it.

"If you're not showering," Ms. Puff was saying, "just say, 'O.B.' That means you're observing." Then she laughed and said, "Be sure not to say 'B.O.'!" She laughed louder now.

"B.O.?" said Sara. "What's that?"

Ginger leaned over to her. "Body odor," she whispered.

Sara giggled nervously and rolled her eyes.

"The rest of you, get undressed," Ms. Puff ordered. "Come on, people. Let's go!"

I didn't move.

I didn't want to take my clothes off!

I'd already seen everybody in their underwear. That was bad enough, everyone sort of checking everybody else out, who needed bras and who didn't.

But now everyone would really be able to see *everything* and—well, you know—kind of—*compare.*

We walked back to our lockers and slowly started to undress. I looked at the floor so I wouldn't look at anyone. I hoped everyone else was doing the same.

I didn't want to be the first person without clothes, though, so I peeked up a little so I'd end up naked about the same time everyone else did.

I kept staring at the floor. It was hard to do that, though, when we all lined up to tell Ms. Puff our names. I kept my head down, but glanced up twice so I wouldn't bump into anyone. It would be horrible to bump into a naked person.

We probably set Guinness speed records for shower taking—I bet not one bar of soap got wet—and hurried back to our lockers and got dressed.

Nobody talked the whole time. Not one peep out of anybody!

Then it was over.

Gradually, the talking started up again.

I was relieved—until I realized I'd have to take a shower next week and the week after that. I'd have to take a shower after every single gym class until the end of the year.

I'd never thought that my favorite class would turn out to be something I'd dread.

I wasn't sure I could stand it.

"How was school today, honey?"

Mom padded barefoot around the kitchen getting supper ready. Dad was sitting in the living room watching the news.

Dad sells insurance downtown, and Mom teaches piano at Withmore College. They get home about the same time and take turns fixing dinner. I like Dad's nights best because he fixes the food I like: hamburgers, baked chicken, lasagna, normal stuff.

Mom, on the other hand, likes to fix us healthy meals, like vegetarian stew with oat-bran muffins or tofu stir-fry over brown rice.

Sometimes it takes all I've got to choke down that stuff.

"School was okay." I shrugged. I didn't want to go into it. "What's for supper?"

"A new recipe," Mom said. "Buckwheat pancakes—"

"Wow," I said. "That sounds good." I almost said "for once" but stopped myself just in time.

"With prune whip sauce."

"Prune whip sauce?"

"It sounds wonderful," Mom said cheerfully, hurrying to the refrigerator. "And it's filled with vitamins, fiber, calcium, and essential fatty acids."

"Great."

"Remember, our bodies are—"

"—like fine-tuned machinery," I finished with her.

This was definitely a night for my Ban All Revolting Food plan.

I use the B.A.R.F. plan, which I call it for short, only in times of crisis. It has two parts: (1) getting rid of mom's healthy food; and (2) eating something good. Both parts require planning and a certain amount of sneakiness.

Part One is sometimes hard, sometimes easy. Cracked bulgar wheat or lentil nut loaf, for instance, are easy to get rid of. I just hide them in the cuffs or the waistband of my shorts. Then when I leave the table, I go to the bathroom and flush them down the toilet.

Getting rid of something like asparagus soup is a lot trickier. Sometimes I get my dog, Bob, to eat it.

Sometimes, though, even Bob hates it. I can't blame him. Then I have to pretend I'm suddenly sick so I can be excused from the table.

I don't like having to resort to these low-down tricks, but when you're faced with okra and brussels sprout surprise, drastic measures are sometimes necessary.

The second part of the B.A.R.F Plan is easier. A lot of times I get myself invited over to Zach's house after dinner. Zach's mom is a dessert freak and makes something gooey and delicious every night.

I watched Mom dump a can of prunes into the blender and turn it on. It whipped around the plastic container in a blur of brown liquid that turned my stomach to look at.

I sure hoped Bob liked prunes.

"Please call everyone to the table, Lizard," Mom said a few minutes later. "Dinner's ready."

I yelled at everyone to come, then hurried back to the kitchen. I poured milk as Dad and Sam sat down.

"What's this?" Dad asked when Mom brought in the platter.

"Buckwheat cakes," Mom said. "With prune whip sauce."

Dad's eyebrows shot up. "Sounds interesting." He's a jock, like my mom, and very conscious of his health. He just isn't a nut about it the way Mom is.

Sam groaned and sat down.

"You'll love it," Mom said. She always pretends she doesn't hear the complaints about her meals.

I took the milk back to the refrigerator, then hurried to the cupboard and grabbed a small dish, which I shoved under my shirt.

I walked back into the dining room and sat down.

"Dig in, guys!" Mom said, cutting her cakes with a fork.

She turned to Sam. "How did football practice go today?"

"Tough," he said. "Coach Barnhart's into torture and cruelty."

"I could take the physical torture," I said.

"It's the mental cruelty I can do without. He's such a jerk."

"He wants everyone to work hard," Sam said.

"He doesn't have to yell and scream and call kids names."

"He gets results," Sam said. "We've got the best middle-school football team in this part of the state."

"I still say Barnhart's a jerk," I said. "You couldn't get me on his team if you gave me a million dollars."

"Nobody'd give you a million dollars to play football," Sam said, grinning. "Besides, Barnhart wouldn't let a girl on the team, anyway."

"Even if she was the best player to try out?"

"Yeah, but you wouldn't be, because *I'd* be the best player to try out!"

"You wish."

"Okay, enough," Mom said, holding up her hands.

"What position will you play?" Dad asked.

"Maybe wide receiver," Sam said. "Coach watches me a lot when we practice passing and receiving."

71

"Who'll quarterback for your first game?" I asked.

"Maybe Al Pickering," he said. "Or Tom Luther."

"When is it?" Mom asked. "We want to come."

Sam pulled a piece of folded paper out of his pocket. "Here's the schedule."

He handed it to Mom, who leaned over and studied the dates with Dad.

Now was my chance.

I pulled the dish out of my shirt, cut a huge piece out of my buckwheat cakes and scooped it into the dish.

I pushed the dish under the table. Bob was sitting in the corner of the dining room. I drummed my fingers on the side of my chair to get his attention.

Then I looked up. Sam was staring right at me. *Uh-oh*, I thought.

Sam started to speak, then closed his mouth. He got a funny look in his eye and gave me a tiny smile.

Bob trotted over to me and sniffed the cakes. In a minute, he had devoured all of them. He slobbered a little on my bare leg, but that was okay. Better to have prune whip on my leg than in my mouth. Bob trotted back into his corner, licking his chops.

Sam continued to watch me. "Who's your locker partner, Lizard?" His voice was super-casual.

"A girl named Ginger Flush," I said. "She's a nincompoop."

Mom and Dad were still looking over the schedule and murmuring about the dates.

"Other than that," Sam said, "what's she like?"

"She's stupid," I said. "Why do you want to know?"

"Just wondered. She talked to me in the hall. She said you two were locker partners."

"So why'd you ask?" I said. "By the way, she has a crush on you. She says you're a fox."

Sam shifted in his chair and looked away for a minute.

It was fun watching him squirm.

"She wanted me to put in a good word for her."

"Yeah?" Sam said. He grinned. "Cool."

"What?"

"That's cool, she thinks I'm a fox."

"Are you nuts?" I said. "Ginger Flush is a grade-A, blue-ribbon airhead!"

Sam shrugged. "She seems okay to me."

Mom turned to us. "Who's an airhead?"

Sam glared at me.

I ignored him. "Sam wants to know about this girl—"

"What girl?" Mom asked.

"Here, Bob!" Sam called out. He whistled. "Lizard has a treat for you!"

Bob came running right to me under the table.

"What girl?" Mom asked again. "What are you giving Bob, Lizard?"

At the same time Sam said, "Never mind," and I said, "Nothing."

Sam and I glowered at each other.

Truce. We didn't have to say it out loud, but we both knew it. I wouldn't tell about Ginger; he wouldn't tell that I gave my dinner to Bob.

"Oh, Lizard," Mom said, smiling. "You've nearly finished your pancakes already! Would you like some more?"

"No, thank you," I said politely.

"Sam," she said, looking at his plate, "you've got a ways to go."

Sam hadn't even touched his plate.

He scowled at me, and I smiled back very sweetly.

"Your mom makes the best chocolate cake on

the planet," I said.

"She sure does," Zach said.

We sat on the top step of his back porch in the fading light, devouring humongous slabs of cake and piles of ice cream. My mom would've had plenty to say about the cholesterol and saturated fat we were shoving in our faces. I say, if it tastes good, who cares?

Bob and Klondike sat at our feet, gazing up at us. Occasionally, one of them would whimper.

"I could swear Bob practices that pitiful look when I'm not around," I said.

"He does," Zach said. "As soon as you leave for school, he runs up to your room, sits on your bed, and practices in front of the mirror."

I grinned. "And how would you know that?"

"He told Klondike, and Klondike can't keep a secret."

I laughed and took the last bite of chocolate cake. Then I put the plate down for Bob and Klondike to lick clean. Zach did, too.

We leaned against the porch railing and looked up at the sky. "A blanket of stars," Zach said.

"Do you think there's intelligent life on

other planets?" I asked.

"I know there's life, but I wouldn't call it intelligent."

I grinned. "How come?"

"I've seen the aliens."

"When was that?"

"It was about ten days ago," he said, leaning forward and resting his elbows on his knees. "Klondike and I woke up about two in the morning, and my room was as bright as day. I went to my window, and hovering over the treetops was a huge, round ship with bright lights running around the edge."

"What did you do?" I asked.

"I pulled on my jeans, and Klondike and I went outside." Zach pointed to a large maple tree next to the garage. "Standing under the tree were two aliens. One of them came over and looked Klondike in the eyes and started making noises.

"I realized that the alien thought Klondike was the master and *I* was the pet. He touched Klondike's head, and before you could blink, we were all transported to the spaceship. He fed Klondike and me some blue food that tasted like cheese enchiladas.

"'Zach, when do we get to go home?' a

voice said. I didn't hear it with my ears; it came from inside my head. I looked at Klondike and realized he was talking to me!

"I figured the food made us able to communicate with each other, mind-to-mind. The alien came over and mentally said to Klondike, 'Is this your only human or do you have a herd?'

"This had to be the dumbest alien in the universe," Zach said. "So I decided to show him that I was Klondike's boss. I said, 'Sit, Klondike. Speak. Roll over.'"

"Did he do his tricks?" I asked.

"No," Zach said. "Klondike said to the alien, 'Get a load of this pet, telling me what to do.' Then he laughed."

"Klondike laughed?" I said.

"His laugh sounds like Elmer Fudd in the cartoons, sort of like this: huh-huh-huh-huh-huh."

"How did you get away from the aliens?" I asked.

"Simple. I promised them Klondike's first-born son."

"I thought Klondike was fixed," I said.

"He is."

I laughed. Zach sat back, grinning, and

relaxed against the rail. "Maybe I'll be a writer when I grow up. Either that or a professional baseball player."

Klondike ran up the porch steps, wagging his tail, and licked Zach's face. Bob watched, wagging his own tail.

"That's a great story," I said. "You should tell the kids at school."

"Yeah, maybe." He paused. "You see the posters for the dance next week?"

I sighed. I'd heard more about that stupid dance in the past few days than I ever wanted to hear in a lifetime.

"Yeah. I'm not wasting my time with it."

"Mmm."

"You don't want to go, do you?"

"Well," Zach said, "I s'pose it's a way to get to know the new people better."

"What new people?"

"The kids from other elementary schools."

"I think the friends I have now are the best," I said. "I don't need to have more friends."

Zach scratched behind Klondike's ear. "It's good to have lots of friends."

My stomach was turning sour again. "You never needed more friends before now," I said.

My voice was starting to sound whiney. I cleared my throat and lowered it as much as I could. "I don't get it."

Zach shrugged. "It might be fun."

"Dancing?"

"Or not dancing. Just talking."

"You can talk to people at school between classes," I said.

Zach didn't say any more about it. He got up and grabbed a stick on the ground. "Come on, Klondike. Come on, Bob," he said. "Let's play fetch."

I watched Zach and the dogs run around the yard. I didn't feel like joining them. What had gotten into my old pal? First, he didn't seem to mind Lisa and Ginger practically drooling all over him. And now he said he might like to go to that stupid school dance! This was not the Zach I thought I knew.

I got up to go home. My stomach was killing me.

I lay on my bed and stared up at the ceiling. I'd been thinking about Zach, but there was something else bothering me. I hadn't wanted to think about it, but it kept nudging me from a corner of my mind. It was what Ms. Puff had said in gym class.

If you're having your period, you don't have to shower.

Why was that?

I knew what menstruation was. We'd had a film about it in fourth grade.

The film went into a lot of technical stuff about the ovaries, eggs, and uterus and explained why menstruation happens. But it didn't answer a lot of important questions, like: When would I get my period for the first time? Where would it happen? At school? When I'm sleeping? When I'm playing ball with the guys?

Guys are so lucky, I thought. *They never have to deal with anything like this.* It was so unfair.

I put my hands behind my head and thought about the commercials I'd seen on TV. Somehow I couldn't see myself walking on the beach with my mother discussing cramping and bloating.

The last time we'd talked about it, I was sort of embarrassed, and I could tell she was, too. She asked me if I had questions, and when I said I didn't, she seemed relieved.

But I did have questions. Lots of them.

I got up and walked out of my room, down the hallway, and into the bathroom. I closed the door behind me.

A large closet stands just inside the door. I opened it and looked around. Maybe I'd find whatever Mom uses. Maybe there would be directions on the box.

I pushed aside some junk—a jar of Vaseline, a collection of hairbrushes, bottles of aspirin and cough syrup. Behind that, at the back of the closet, sat a cup that Sam had won at the Washington Elementary fair. Inside the cup was a razor; next to the cup was a can of shaving foam.

"Why would Sam—" Then it hit me. *Sam's shaving?*

Sam, with the baby-soft skin, thinks he needs to shave? What a ridiculous thought!

I kept looking for what I'd come here to find. On the second shelf, I found something that looked promising. It was a blue box with little white flowers on it. Inside were long, thin, paper-wrapped things.

I unwrapped one of them and stared at it. "What the heck is this?" I said.

"What?"

I jumped. The voice was coming from the hall.

I crammed everything back into the closet and opened the door. Sam stood there in the hall.

"What are you doing?" he said. "Who are you talking to?"

"No one," I said. I could feel my face getting hot and prickly.

"You looking for something?"

"None of your business!" Then I remembered why he wanted to know. "If you're worried about your *shaving* equipment, I left it where I found it. I'm sure you'll want to shave off that duckling fuzz on your face!"

"You got into my stuff!" he yelled. "You leave my stuff alone!"

"You can have your stupid shaving stuff," I said. "I'm sure you want to look nice for Ginger the Airhead!"

I stalked into my room and slammed the door. I leaned against it till my heart calmed down.

Sam, shaving? I couldn't believe how stupid he was sometimes.

And what was that thing I'd found in the blue box?

I'm going to have to ask Mary Ann, I thought. She has an older sister, so she must know all about this stuff.

Actually, I really didn't want to know all about it. But it was a lot scarier not knowing.

7

I had my questions for Mary Ann all ready the next morning. I'd written them out the night before and memorized them. Then I tore the paper into a thousand pieces and threw the pieces into the wastebasket.

As I rode my bike, I mentally went over my questions for the millionth time:

1. *When do girls get their periods?*
2. *How much does it hurt?*
3. *Does a period start suddenly and gush out, making a red splotch on your clothes?*

I thought I'd act very casual and sort of ease into the subject by talking about my P.E. class.

Mary Ann had called me last night to ask if we could ride by ourselves today without the guys. She didn't say why, but I was glad. There was no way I could find out what I needed to know with them around.

Mary Ann had told me she'd meet me at the bridge. I slowed down a little and looked around for her, but I couldn't see her. Another girl was standing there next to her bike. She was probably waiting for someone.

The girl on the bridge waved. I squinted.

It was Mary Ann!

"You really did it!" I called out. I sped up to the bridge and then stopped right in front of her. "You got scalped!"

Her face fell, and she touched her short hair. "Don't you like it?"

I looked at it more carefully.

"It's so different."

"Different good or different bad?" she asked.

"Maybe you're not even the real Mary Ann. Maybe you're an imposter. You kidnapped Mary Ann again, didn't you? What have you done with her?" I looked down at her legs. "At least you're not still trying the panty hose disguise."

Mary Ann looked anxious. "I thought it looked kind of nice." She looked back at me. "You don't like it, do you?"

"I don't care how it looks. Just give me my friend back."

"It's really easy to take care of," she said. "I can just blow it dry in a couple of minutes." She glanced sideways at me. "Do you think I look older with my hair like this?"

"Older?" I said. "Why would you want to look older?"

"I don't know. But do you think I do?"

"Maybe a couple of months. But I still think you're a fake."

She huffed loudly so I'd know she was ticked off. "Nice, Lizard," she said. "Really nice!" She turned her bike toward school and we headed off.

While we were riding, I sneaked peeks at her. It was weird seeing Mary Ann look so different. Why would she want to look older?

I hadn't forgotten about the questions I wanted to ask her. It's just that I wasn't in the mood anymore to ask her about them.

Boy, Mary Ann's hair was the hot topic of the

day. I don't know what all the fuss was about. You'd think she had won a gold medal at the Olympics or something instead of just getting her hair cut.

It started as soon as we arrived at school. We were locking our bikes to the rack, and I heard this loud squeal.

"Oh, look at Mary Ann! Oooooo! Her hair's wonderful!"

I looked up as a group of girls hurried over. They weren't Ginger's squealer friends, but they were just like them.

"Oh, Mary Ann! It's totally fabulous!" gushed a girl with long blond hair.

"Who did it?" cooed another girl who fingered Mary Ann's short locks. "I've got to get an appointment."

"Her name is Tracy," Mary Ann said, beaming. "She's at Hair Unlimited."

"The boys will really go after you now," said a third girl.

"And that blush is wonderful!" the blonde said. "What's the shade?"

Mary Ann giggled. "Coy Pink."

Blush? Mary Ann was wearing blush?

The bell rang then and the squealers hurried off.

"You're wearing blush?" I said. I peered at

her cheeks. "Why would you want to do that?"

"I don't have much on. Tracy put it on me, and I kind of liked it. Do you?"

"I didn't even know you had it on," I said.

"That's how it's supposed to look—like it's not even there."

"If it's not supposed to show, why bother?" I said.

"Are you mad or something?"

"Why should I be mad?" My voice sounded loud.

"I don't know," she said. "You're just acting funny."

"No, I'm not mad," I said.

Maybe I *was* mad, just a little. I guess it was because Mary Ann was doing the things that those dumb girly-girls do. And we hate girly-girls.

At least I thought we did.

I did.

When I got to my locker, I found two pink envelopes stuck to it with tape. One was labeled "Ginger" and the other was for me. I tore mine off the locker and opened it.

The card had three pink bunnies on the outside. It said, "Please hop on over to my party!" On the inside were lines that had been filled in.

What: *A slumber party!*
When: *Saturday night, 8 P.M.*
Where: *At Lisa's house, 2113 Oakcrest Drive*

Lisa had written on the bottom in her loopy handwriting: *Bring a sleeping bag and pillow. We'll provide the movie, the munchies, and the soda. Be prepared NOT to sleep.*

I tossed the invitation back into my locker and pulled out the books I'd need for the morning.

"Hi, Lizard!" Ginger appeared behind me with Heather and Tiffany.

Ginger ripped her envelope off the locker door. "This must be Lisa's party invitation." She pulled out the card. "That's cute." She held up the card for Heather and Tiffany to see. "It'll be a great party. Can you go?" she asked me.

"How did you know I was invited?"

"Lisa told me. You and Mary Ann are both invited. Hey, we saw Mary Ann's hair this morning! She looks adorable!"

"Really cute," Tiffany said.

"Sophisticated," Heather said.

"She's smart." Ginger smiled knowingly. "She's making herself into boy bait."

"Into *what?*"

"You know," Ginger said. "Boy bait. She's going to attract the boys in a major way. Wait till they see her today."

"What are you talking about?"

"Her new hairdo," Ginger said patiently. "Her new look. The new cut and blush. She's obviously doing it to get boys."

"She looks older with her hair like that," Heather said.

"Maybe she'll even get an *eighth grader,*" Ginger said. "That would be *spectacular.*"

I had a headache. "I gotta go to class."

"Okay, see you later," Ginger said.

"'Bye, Lizard!" Heather and Tiffany said.

I turned and hurried down the hall. Was Ginger right? Was Mary Ann doing all that stuff to turn herself into boy bait? My head was filled with all the stuff I'd seen and heard since school had started. Everything was different. People were acting so weird.

I stopped in the recessed doorway to an empty room and watched the students walk by. They looked normal; they talked and laughed and hurried by.

But they weren't normal.

I remembered an old movie I'd seen on TV about aliens that take over the Earth. In a horrible process called The Change, the aliens turned everyone into zombies, one by one.

This is like an alien takeover, I thought. The aliens were getting everyone in town! First Zach, then Mary Ann and Sam. And all the rest of the kids who looked and acted different from last year. They were going through The Change, and there was nothing I could do to stop it. It was spreading through town, out of control.

Well, they didn't have me. And they weren't going to get me. I wouldn't let them. I'd be the last normal kid remaining on the planet.

Alone against the aliens.

8

"Why would you want to go to that slumber party?" I said to Mary Ann in the hall between classes. "Those girls are so stupid! And Lisa's a snot!"

She'd just run over to tell me she'd been invited. The hallway was crowded. Kids flowed past us as we stood in the middle like a couple of rocks in a rushing stream.

"I know they're kind of silly," Mary Ann said. "But I like them anyway. Maybe it's dumb, but I like being a part of the group. Besides, they're a lot of fun."

"Fun?" I said loudly. "Hairstyles and dances

and *boys*! That's fun? Who cares about that stuff?"

Mary Ann looked embarrassed when I started yelling. She pulled me over next to the wall. "What's wrong with liking those things?" she said. She looked mad now.

"Mary Ann, what's gotten into you?"

"What are you talking about?"

"You're turning into somebody I don't even know," I said. "Wearing panty hose, cutting your hair—"

"Things are different now," Mary Ann said. "We're not little kids anymore." She took a step back and raised her voice. "And stop talking as if I'm not being a loyal friend just because I bought a pair of tights!"

"You're turning into the *enemy*," I said.

"What?"

"You're turning into a stupid girly-girl who runs with the airhead crowd and does everything everyone else does. *You're turning into a zombie, Mary Ann!*"

"Well, thank you very much!"

"Those girls are idiots!"

"So stay home by yourself!" Mary Ann snapped. "But you won't make any friends that way. And if you're not careful, Lizard

Flanagan, you're not going to have any friends left!"

She turned and stalked down the hall.

I watched her go. The corridor had pretty much cleared by now. Most of the kids were at their next class.

I waited for Mary Ann to turn back and look at me, but she didn't. She kept walking.

I suddenly felt very lonely. Mary Ann and I'd had fights before, but this time was different. I shouldn't have called her a zombie, but it was too late to take it back.

I felt a hollow sensation in the pit of my stomach. Maybe I'd have to go to that stupid slumber party. Not because I wanted to, but because I didn't want Mary Ann to be mad at me forever and ever.

"Sam, I need the sleeping bag," I said, opening his bedroom door on Friday afternoon.

Sam's head jerked up from a magazine he was reading. He slid it under his pillow and jumped from the bed.

"It's right here," he said. He hurried to his closet and pulled the sleeping bag out of the back.

"What were you reading?" I asked.

"What?"

"The magazine. The one you shoved under your pillow."

I walked over to his bed and pulled it out from under the pillow before he reached me.

"Leave my stuff alone!" he yelled.

The cover showed a woman wearing a thong swimsuit looking back over her shoulder toward the camera, her hair blowing in the breeze.

"*Sports Illustrated*—the swimsuit issue," I said.

"That's none of your business!" Sam yelled. "Get out of my room!"

"Why are you looking at this?"

"I've been reading *Sports Illustrated* for years!"

"But this is September," I said. "Why are you reading the February issue?"

"Give it back!" He grabbed at the magazine, but I yanked my arm back.

"This isn't Mom's issue," I said. "The address label says Howard Mechtensteimer. Have you guys been passing this around, *leering* at it?"

"So what?" He spat the words at me. "I missed that issue when it came out."

"I think you're disgusting!" I shouted. "You dirty-minded—"

Sam threw himself at me and tackled me. We fell backward onto the bed. He grabbed for the magazine, but I held it as far away as I could.

"Give it to me!" he yelled.

"You make me sick!" I yelled back.

He leaped forward and grabbed hold of the magazine, but I held on tight.

R-i-i-p!

Sam held several pages of the magazine in his fist. "Look what you did!" he hollered. "Give me the magazine!"

"Stop grabbing at it!"

He lunged for it again and tore out some more pages. He looked at the paper in his hands. "You ripped it! It doesn't even belong to me!" He picked up the sleeping bag and shoved it at me. "Get out of my room!" he screamed.

"My pleasure," I said. "You're sickening, you . . . you *zombie!*"

I yanked the sleeping bag from him and stomped down the hall to my room.

"This is going to be horrible," I said to Mary Ann on the way to Lisa's slumber party. We were both walking down the sidewalk carrying sleeping bags with our p.j.'s and toothbrushes rolled up inside.

"It won't be horrible," Mary Ann said. "Just you wait. You'll be surprised and glad you changed your mind about coming. These girls seem really nice." She looked at the houses around us. "What's the number?"

I pushed my sleeping bag under my right arm and fished a small piece of paper out of my jeans pocket.

"Um, 2113 Oakcrest."

"There it is, up ahead," Mary Ann said.

It was a big white house with green shutters and a green roof. Some red flowers were growing in window boxes under the downstairs windows.

"Nice," Mary Ann said.

We walked up the front walk and knocked on the door.

In a few seconds, it was yanked open. Crowded into the doorway were Lisa, Ginger, Tiffany, Heather, and Sara.

"Come in," Lisa said. "Now we're all here."

"We're going to have a BLAST! A FANTAZMIC party!" Ginger said. "Dump your sleeping bags in the living room. That's where we're not sleeping!"

We went into the living room, tossed our stuff on the floor, and sat down.

"What are we going to do first, Lisa?" Heather asked.

"What do you think?" Ginger answered. "Eat! Right, Lisa?"

"Right," Lisa said. She jumped up. "Popcorn's all made. You guys come and choose your drinks."

We followed Lisa into the large kitchen. A kettle was sitting on the kitchen counter, filled with popcorn. It smelled terrific, and it glistened with melted butter. Next to it were bowls full of M&M's and Hot Tamales. My mother would've been horrified.

"You've got your choice of Pepsi, Diet Pepsi, root beer, or 7 Up," Lisa said.

"I'd better go with the diet," Ginger said.

"Me, too," Heather said, and all the rest of the girls piled onto the Diet Pepsi bandwagon.

"I'll have a root beer," I said.

Ginger grinned. "You work off all those calories with sports," she said. "Playing with the boys."

"I think I could learn to like sports," Lisa said. She smiled slyly.

"Especially if hunky Zach was around," Ginger added.

The girls laughed and looked at me. I nodded and tried to smile.

"So, Lizard," Lisa said, plunking ice into the glasses, "tell us about him."

"About Zach?" I said.

Lisa turned to me. That cool smile was still on her lips. "Of course, about Zach."

"What do you want to know?"

"Well—" Lisa thought a moment. "What's his favorite color?"

"I don't know," I said.

Lisa frowned. "Well, what does he like to do?" She poured root beer into the first glass.

"Play baseball and football," I said.

"What else?"

The root beer fizz climbed up the glass and started to pour over the top. I stuck my finger in it, and it died back a little.

"He likes to camp," I said. I licked my finger. "He and his dad go to the boundary waters every year to camp and fish."

Lisa nodded.

"Ask the most important question," Ginger said, nudging Lisa.

"Lay off, Ginge. I'm getting to it," Lisa said. "What kind of girls does he like?"

What a stupid question. Why didn't she ask what kind of people Zach likes?

"Athletic ones," I said, knowing how she'd feel about that.

Lisa's face fell. "Really?"

"Yeah."

Seeing her disappointment was great.

Lisa rolled her eyes. "I suppose I'm going to have to learn more about football and baseball."

"Good idea!" said Ginger. "Maybe we should all bone up on this sports thing. There's a high school football game coming up. I bet all the boys will be there. I bet Sam will go, right?"

I shrugged. "Sure. We always go."

"Speaking of the game," Lisa said, "I have a surprise announcement to make." She paused dramatically. "I'm going to be in the first football game. Well, at halftime, anyway."

Ginger gasped. "Doing what?"

"The theme for halftime is Hawaii," Lisa said, smiling. Her eyes were shining with excitement. "My class at the dance studio has been invited to dance the hula in front of the band!"

The girls shrieked.

"Will you wear a grass skirt?" Ginger asked.

"No, we're wearing short wrap skirts and halter tops," Lisa said. "We started learning the steps tonight after school."

"Are you nervous?" Heather asked.

"I'd be a wreck!" Tiffany said.

"I'm okay," Lisa said.

Of course. Was she ever not cool?

"Wow, you'll get Zach for sure now!" Ginger said. "You'll be a celebrity!"

"That's true," Lisa said, pouring Diet Pepsi into the other glasses.

That little smile was still on her face, and I wanted to smack it right off.

We went back to the living room and sat on the floor.

"What are you guys wearing to the dance next week?" Heather asked.

"I got a cute sweater and skirt just for the dance," Ginger said.

"I have a pair of cream-colored leggings and a *very* short lemon skirt," Lisa said. She grinned and threw her long mane of hair over one shoulder. "I don't mean to brag, but I look really good in it."

I looked at Mary Ann and made a face, but she pretended she didn't see.

"I can't wait," Ginger said, giggling. "I keep dreaming about what it'll be like. The music will be playing, and Sam the Fox will come over and ask me to dance. Boy, would I like to get romantic with him!"

I felt like throwing up.

"Just thinking about slow dancing with a boy gives me the shivers," Sara said.

"Me too," Tiffany said, and they both squealed.

"I have this nightmare sometimes," Sara confided. "What if I go to the dance and everybody's dancing—except me?" She covered her face with her hands. "I'd just die."

"Me, too," Ginger said. "If Sam doesn't ask me to dance, I'll just have to ask him!"

"It would be too embarrassing to stand around because nobody wanted to dance with you," said Heather. "I couldn't show my face at school for a week!"

I couldn't believe how important this stupid dance was to these girls. It made me sick.

"I hope Zach asks me to dance," Lisa said.

"Who do you want to dance with, Mary Ann?" Heather asked.

Mary Ann's face got red. "I don't know." She glanced over at me, then looked down at the Diet Pepsi in her hand.

"Don't you have a crush on anybody?" Ginger asked.

"Well—" She bit her lip. "No."

As I mentioned before, Mary Ann is a rotten liar.

"Yes, you do!" all the girls shrieked at once. "Who is it?"

"Yes, Mary Ann," I said. *"Who?"*

"Nobody," she insisted. Her face was really red and for a second I thought she might cry.

There was an awkward silence.

"Who do you want to dance with, Lizard?" Ginger asked.

"I'm not going."

"What!" they all said. "Why not?"

"It'll be boring."

The girls were stunned. They looked at me as if *I* was the alien, which was kind of funny considering what I thought of them.

"Wow," Ginger said. "How could anybody think a dance would be boring?"

"Pass the popcorn, will you?" I said to Lisa, even though I didn't feel like eating it.

Lisa handed me the popcorn. Then she picked up a pile of magazines from a small table.

"These magazines all have makeovers," she said, passing them around. "They take plain-looking girls and do these miraculous make-overs and the girls turn out *beautiful.*"

I flipped through my magazine till I found the makeover page. I stared at the pictures. The woman in the "before" picture sure didn't look like the same person in the "after" picture. Of course, in the "before" picture she also looked like she needed a shower.

"We should send these anonymously to Shannon and her uncool friends," Lisa said. "Have you seen those clothes they wear? They might as well wear sacks!"

"Yeah," Ginger said. "Over their heads!"

The girls roared.

"Lizard, tell me about Sam," Ginger said.

"You mean like, what's his favorite color?" I said it sarcastically, but she didn't seem to notice.

"Anything."

"Well—he once made a belch last for eight seconds." The girls howled. "Eight seconds! That's gross!"

At least they weren't talking about romance anymore.

"Speaking of setting records," Sara said. "You know Meg Small?"

"Yeah," Mary Ann said. "She's in most of my classes."

Sara nodded. "Yeah, well, she got her period at the beginning of fifth grade!" She grinned. "You notice how quiet everyone got in gym class when Puff said we didn't have to shower if we had our period?"

The girls laughed.

"My sister says that Ms. Puff counts out the days between the times you say you're observing," Mary Ann said. "If it's less than twenty-eight days, she thinks you're lying and lowers your grade."

"You're kidding," Heather said. "That's not fair."

"I heard that, too," Ginger said. "Last year a girl was helping Ms. Puff in her office, and she saw Puff doing exactly that."

"My cousin gets her period every eighteen days," Tiffany said.

"That poor girl!" said Ginger.

"Yeah, but it's unfair for Ms. Puff to lower your grade if you really *do* get your period every eighteen days," said Tiffany.

"Maybe she'll make you get a note from your doctor to prove you're telling the truth," said Mary Ann.

I couldn't imagine having to talk to Ms. Puff about something like that. I couldn't even imagine talking to my doctor about it.

"I just don't want to get my period during school," Ginger said. "I've been praying a lot about that."

"Wouldn't it be horrible?" said Mary Ann.

Ginger nodded. "There was a girl in my sister's class who started her period right in Mr. Maloney's class. I mean, she was bleeding hard."

"Oh, no!" everyone gasped.

"I'd just die if Mr. Maloney knew I'd started my period," Sara said.

I was horrified. What an awful thing to happen to a person! How could you show your face at school after that?

I felt a panicky feeling rising in my chest. Was there anything I could do to make sure that would never happen to me?

Lisa played a movie on the VCR after that, but I couldn't concentrate on it. For the next few hours, even after the others had finally fallen asleep, I kept thinking about starting my period.

Everything seemed so out of control. I could keep myself from turning into a zombie. That was no problem. But there was something in me that would change, whether I liked it or not, and I couldn't do a thing about it.

I hoped I'd get my period while I was at home. And I decided that from now on, I'd keep a sweatshirt in my locker. I'd carry it around with me every day, even if it was a hundred degrees outside. Then if I started my period really hard, I'd tie it around my waist to cover up the red spot.

When I finally fell asleep, I dreamed about aliens taking over the brains of people on Earth.

9

The living room was empty. Now was my chance. I went to the bookcase, selected the *M* book from the set of encyclopedias, tucked it under my arm, and took the stairs two at a time up to my room.

"Menstruation, menstruation," I mumbled, leafing through the pages. "Here it is."

A diagram took up most of the page. It showed the uterus, fallopian tubes, ovaries, egg, the whole bit. I'd seen all that in the film in fourth grade, and I wasn't particularly interested. What I really needed to know were the answers to my questions.

I scanned the article, but it didn't say much.

A couple of sentences near the end of the article caught my eye.

> During the time of blood flow, some women wear a **pad** or **feminine napkin**. Other women choose to use a **tampon**, made of absorbent material, which is worn internally.

A tampon. That had to be what that long, thin thing was that was in the bathroom. Yuck. I decided I'd use a pad when the time came.

I closed the encyclopedia and shoved it under my school books. I'd take it downstairs when I knew everyone was gone.

But the unanswered questions were replaying in my head, over and over: *When* would it come? And *how*?

I flopped on my bed and buried my face in the pillow. Being a girl sure wasn't as easy as it had been in elementary school.

For the next week, the girls talked constantly about the dance on Friday after school. They debated about what to wear, who would be there, how to fix their hair, and mostly who would ask them to dance.

I tried to tune it out, but it wasn't easy. I

was surrounded by it.

"Have you changed your mind about the dance?" Mary Ann asked before the bell starting school on Friday. We hadn't mentioned it since the slumber party.

"Nope."

"All the guys will be there," she said.

"I bet not," I said. "We rode all the way to school with them today, and no one even brought it up. Zach's the only one who's talked about it at all. He didn't say for sure he was going, and he hasn't said a word about it since."

"Sam hasn't mentioned it?"

"Nope," I said again.

"That's strange. Maybe they don't know about it."

"There're posters up all over school. They couldn't have missed them."

"So you're definitely not going?" she said.

"Nope."

"Well, I guess I'll go with Ginger then."

"Suit yourself."

I'd wondered who Mary Ann was hoping to dance with. I decided I didn't want to know.

Mary Ann was wearing a new pair of dressy shorts and a white shirt. She hadn't worn a skirt since the first day of school.

Most of the girls were dressed up, wearing new walking shorts or skirts or even dresses. Before and after classes, the girls talked and laughed louder than usual. They stood in groups in the halls and whispered excitedly to one another and stared at the boys and sometimes yelled flirty comments at them. The guys were just as bad, yelling stuff back and grinning like idiots. It was all pretty disgusting.

"I can't wait to dance with Zach," Lisa whispered to me during gym class. It was raining outside, so we were getting ready to play volleyball. Ms. Puff had just finished taking roll. Mr. Grodin, standing in front of the boys on the other side of the gym, was taking roll, too.

"I don't think Zach will be there," I said.

A look of horror passed over Lisa's face. "But he said he was going."

I stared at her. "He did?"

"Yeah," Lisa said. "Ginger asked him about it on Wednesday, and he said he was."

I didn't know what to say. He hadn't told me he'd decided to go. Why hadn't he asked me to go with him? He'd always asked me to go to school stuff before.

"In fact, he's going with your brother," Lisa said.

"Sam's going too?"

"*Everybody's* going." Lisa was smirking now. "Didn't they tell you, Lizard?"

I was speechless. Nobody had said a word. Why hadn't they told me?

The volleyball game began. Ed was on my team. All during the first part of the game, I kept glancing him.

"You going to that dance after school?" I finally asked him during a break in the game.

"I don't know," he said. "Maybe. You?"

"No," I said. "Are Sam and Zach going?"

"Maybe," he said. "Why aren't you going?"

I shrugged. "I don't know. Doesn't sound like much fun."

"Yeah," he said. "I know."

"So I'll ride my bike home with you, okay?" I said. "I'll meet you at the bike rack after school."

Ed looked uncomfortable. "Well," he said, "I might go for a few minutes, just to check it out. I don't know."

"Really?"

"Why don't you go, too? All the guys will probably go together."

"Oh."

I didn't want to go to the dance. But I also didn't want to be the only person who didn't go. I didn't like being left out. This was the first time I could remember that ever happening.

"Okay," I said finally. "I'll go and hang out with you guys."

"Okay," Ed said.

A serve came flying over the net. He jumped up and spiked the ball, and we were back in the game.

At least I wasn't going to be the odd man out, I thought. A stupid dance couldn't be that bad. And it would only last for an hour and a half. It wasn't as if I was going to be physically tortured for ninety minutes.

Besides, I kept telling myself, I'd be with my best buddies.

10

After school, the sixth graders headed for the dance in the gym. Lisa was right: everybody was there, practically the whole class. The girls stood along one wall and the boys lined up along the other.

Orange and black crepe paper banners decorated the walls, and orange balloons were tied to chairs lining the room. If the people who'd decorated were going for a romantic look, they'd really blown it. It looked more like a carnival.

I was the only girl on the boys' side, but that was the way I wanted it. I just wished Mary

Ann would've come over to our side.

I had butterflies flying around in my stomach, and that made me pretty ticked off with myself. It was just a stupid dance. *Get a grip, Lizard*, I said to myself.

Mr. Sanders, the lunchroom supervisor, stood behind a long table that had a boom box sitting on it and a microphone on a little stand. He played music, mostly Top 40 stuff from a couple of years ago, and stood there with his hands stuffed into his pockets while the music played. He looked bored.

The music had been playing for about ten minutes, and so far no one had gone out on the floor to dance.

Sam, Zach, Ed, Stinky, and I horsed around with each other. A couple of times every minute, they'd stop and stare across the gym at the girls. On the other side, the girls hollered in one another's ears to be heard over the music. They stared right back at the guys.

At least we weren't dancing. This wasn't too bad. I figured I could handle this for another eighty minutes.

Across the room, a group of girls walked out on the floor. Looking very self-conscious, they started dancing with each other. Everybody watched them.

It was really pathetic. The guys obviously weren't interested in dancing with them, so the girls had to dance with each other.

Too bad. I laughed to myself. I thought about what Sara had said at the slumber party. She'd been worried about being the only girl who wasn't asked to dance. Well, she didn't have to worry about that anymore. No one was asking anyone to dance.

I did sort of feel sorry for Mary Ann, though. But I figured she'd get over the disappointment. Maybe it would help her come to her senses.

I grinned at Zach, who smiled back. "I guess you don't have to dance at a dance," I said. I laughed. "We can talk, just like you said."

He wrestled me into a choke hold and rapped hard on my head with his knuckles.

During the next song, some more girls came out on the floor and danced.

Ed Mechtensteimer punched Zach's arm. "Hey, Walters," he said. "Lisa looks like she wants to dance. Why don't you ask her?"

Zach laughed and shrugged. His ears started to turn red.

"Come on." Ed grinned. "You know she wants you to."

"Not now," Zach said. "I'm talking to Lizard."

"Aw, Zach's shy," Sam said. "Let's help him out."

"Yeah," Ed and Stinky agreed.

"Leave him alone," I said. I pushed Stinky away.

"Hey, don't touch the shirt, Lizard," Stinky said. "I just got this shirt, and it wasn't cheap."

"Give me a break, Stinky. Who cares about your ugly shirt?" I laughed and gave him another shove.

Some of the guys gathered around, grinning.

"This shirt isn't ugly," he insisted. "It's cool."

"Nobody with the name Stinky can be cool." I laughed even louder.

"Hey, how'd you get that name, anyway?" Mike Herman asked.

"He made a stinko in first grade," I told him, "and ever since he's been called Stinky."

We all cracked up.

Except Stinky. His face tensed up hard as a rock. I couldn't tell if he was going to punch me out or run away crying.

I stopped laughing. "Hey, Stinky. I'm sorry. I didn't mean to hurt your feelings."

He gave me a hard shove and walked out of the gym.

The guys moved away from me, glancing at one another. Then they turned and gazed at the other side of the room.

I walked over to Zach.

"Want to go for a walk?" I said. "There's not much going on here."

"No," he said.

"I guess I was too hard on Stinky," I said. "I was just teasing, but I shouldn't have said anything about his name."

"Yeah," he said. He kept his gaze on the other side of the room, then wandered away.

Ed walked over with Mike Herman. "What would you say about Sara Pulliam?" Ed was saying.

Mike looked around. "Where?"

"Over there by the door," Ed said. "The blonde."

"Mmm, I'd give her a seven," Mike said.

"No way, man," Ed said. "Nine plus."

Were they rating her? No, that was too stupid. I leaned in closer.

"I'll show you a nine plus," Mike said. "Look at the girl with the long red hair. She's standing under the basket over there."

"Yeah, I see her," Ed said. "She's okay."

"Okay?" Mike said. "She's terrific! Look at what she does to that sweater!"

He and Ed snickered loudly.

They *were* rating her. It was the most revolting thing I'd ever heard in my life.

"You know what I think?" I butted in. "I think you're both a couple of pigs!"

"What do you mean?" Ed asked.

"You and your sickening ratings," I said. "You guys have turned into a couple of zombies!"

"Pigs or zombies?" Ed shrugged. "Make up your mind."

Mike laughed. They turned their backs on me and went on grading practically every girl in the room.

They hadn't even cared what I thought.

When Zach and Sam came over a few minutes later, Ed and Mike told them what they were doing.

"Lisa's definitely a ten," Zach said. "Maybe an eleven!"

"So's Ginger," Sam said.

So my good buddy Zach and my own brother Sam were just as bad as Ed and Mike. They were all zombies, every one of them.

"You all make me sick," I said.

The guys glanced over at me but didn't say anything.

"If you don't ask Lisa to dance, Walters," Ed said, grinning, "Sam and I will carry you over there!"

"Just cool it," Zach said. "I'll ask her later."

"Let's do it!" Sam said.

They grabbed Zach and dragged him out onto the floor. Zach fought hard, but not too hard, I could tell. Mike Herman joined Sam and Ed, and with three guys against one, there wasn't much Zach could do.

The girls saw them coming and pushed Lisa out in front. She laughed and tossed her hair while her Prince Charming was hauled over to her.

Finally, Zach stood in front of Lisa. I don't think either one of them said anything—their lips didn't move—but after a few seconds, Lisa stepped toward him. Then they started dancing, moving their bodies to the music. The kids hooted and applauded.

I laughed. Zach had never looked sillier, out on that gym floor, trying to dance. He sort of jerked his arms around and then he'd move his feet in little steps while he kept his arms still. It looked as if he couldn't concentrate on his arms and legs at the same time.

When the song was over, I thought Zach would come back to our side. But he didn't. He stayed on the floor with Lisa and started dancing again when a new song started.

I guess Zach gave some of the other guys courage, because about five of them walked over to girls on the other side and asked them to dance.

Al Pickering walked across the floor, right up to Mary Ann. She beamed and they began to dance.

Al Pickering, quarterback on the football team, and Mary Ann! I couldn't believe it. They used to play against each other on the metro flag football league. Now they were *dancing*.

I hadn't seen Mary Ann look this happy since her frog won the Raccoon Creek frog jumping contest in the fourth grade.

Then Sam started across the room.

Oh, no, Sam, not Ginger, I thought as he headed toward my locker partner. *Anybody but Ginger!*

He stopped right in front of her. She nodded and grinned at him, and they started dancing.

I'll have to hear about this at my locker every

day for the rest of the year, I thought.

One by one, the guys on my side of the room walked over and asked girls to dance. Some of the girls came over and invited the guys to dance, too.

Even Ed Mechtensteimer danced. He picked Sara Pulliam, the "nine-plus."

I just stood there and watched. Even Shannon, Angie, and Cheryl were dancing—with one another.

There were only two people in the whole room who weren't dancing. One of them was Mr. Sanders.

And one of them was me.

I walked over to the corner of the room. The volleyball nets had been pushed aside there, and I stood behind them.

What a stupid dance! In fact, everything that had happened since I'd started sixth grade was terrible. I hated middle school!

I looked through the netting at the girls on the other side, and stared at the girls who had received Ed and Mike's highest ratings. On a scale of one to ten, how would the boys rate me?

That's stupid! I thought immediately, shaking the question out of my mind. *Who cares how they would rate me?* It was a rotten way to think about a person.

I looked over at Zach, still dancing with Lisa. He'd rapped on my head hard, and I was still smarting from it.

What a crummy dance, I thought. What a lousy idea, to have a Welcome to Truman Middle School dance.

Some welcome.

And here I was, standing behind the volleyball net.

I suddenly felt really angry, but not at the zombies out on the dance floor. I was steamed at *me*. What was I doing here?

I stepped out from behind the volleyball net and stalked out of the gym. Nobody called me back. Nobody came running after me.

No one even noticed I was gone.

11

"Why'd you leave the dance early?" Mary Ann asked.

She stood at my front door and stared at me through the screen.

"I got bored," I said.

"You should've danced," Mary Ann said. "It was fun."

"You mean by myself?" I said. "That would've been pretty dumb."

"I would have danced with you," Mary Ann said. "A lot of the girls were dancing with other girls."

"Yeah, and they looked pathetic," I said.

"Besides, you were too busy dancing with Al Pickering."

"Are you going to let me in or not?" Mary Ann asked.

"Sure." I opened the screen door. "I have some homework stuff to do," I said.

"On Saturday morning?"

"I like to get it out of the way."

"Since when?"

I didn't answer.

"Lizard," Mary Ann said, "I thought I'd do some shopping for clothes this afternoon. Do you want to come with me?"

"Heck, no. Why would I want to do that?"

"I just thought—well, you don't have to." Mary Ann looked at me a moment without speaking. "See you later," she finally said.

"Okay," I said. Mary Ann turned to go. "Mary Ann?"

She turned back.

"Why do you think none of the guys asked me to dance?"

"Maybe they didn't know you wanted to dance," she said.

"But I know most of them real well," I said. "I play ball with them. Why didn't they even ask me?"

"I don't know," Mary Ann said.

"Did you cut your hair so you'd be boy bait?"

"What?"

"Ginger Flush thinks you cut your hair to get boys interested in you."

"I wanted to look nice," Mary Ann said, "and I wanted boys to ask me to dance. But I cut my hair because I wanted to."

"Good," I said. "I don't want to cut my hair or do anything drastic like that. I just wish somebody—maybe Zach—would've asked me to dance."

"Zach?"

"Yeah," I said. "I don't know why he didn't ask me. I guess he was too busy thinking about Lisa. Do you think she's beautiful?"

"Yes," Mary Ann said. "She's about as beautiful as a person can get."

"But she's not very interesting." I looked at Mary Ann. "Have you ever had the feeling your life is crazy and out of control?"

"What do you mean?"

"Everything around me is changing," I said. I sat on the bottom stair in the foyer. "Everyone is turning into different people, and I can't stop them. I'm the only one who's the same as I was last year." I fiddled with some strands of hair that I hadn't brushed yet today and looked at my toes. "I thought I wanted to stay exactly the same, but now I'm not so sure."

Mary Ann started to say something, but I went on. "I was mean to Stinky yesterday. He left the dance before I did." I rested my elbows on my knees. "Why did I tease him like that?"

"I don't know."

"I'll call him this morning—tell him I'm sorry."

Mary Ann rested her foot on the bottom stair next to me. "I think you'd look nice in a skirt," she said.

I wrinkled my nose. "A *skirt*?"

"Do you want to try one on? Just for fun?"

"What would be fun about trying on a skirt?" She didn't say anything. "Where?"

"Where do you like to get your clothes?"

"The Gap," I said. "Or Sears."

"Great," Mary Ann said. "You want to go to the Gap and look for a denim skirt?"

"No."

"You'd look good in it. And denim is comfortable."

"Well . . . " I guessed it wouldn't hurt to look. "I don't want to do anything drastic."

"Just because you try on a skirt doesn't mean you're going to turn into Ginger Flush."

"Or Lisa St. George," I said. "She's such a

dud. Why would a guy like Zach be interested in her?"

"Probably because she's so pretty."

"But she's not fun or funny—and she doesn't know zilch about sports and is the most unathletic person you'd ever meet in your life!"

"I know."

"It just doesn't make any sense," I said.

"Let's go to the Gap this afternoon," Mary Ann suggested. "We'll find a denim skirt for you."

"Well—I have some money saved from my allowance. But I'm not planning on buying anything. And I won't even *look* at panty hose!"

"Sure." She grinned. "No panty hose."

"This is cute." Mary Ann stopped and looked at the denim skirt on the mannequin. "You like it?"

"It's okay, I guess," I said. "For a skirt. It'd look nicer if it was a pair of jeans."

"May I help you?"

We turned around and saw the saleslady behind us. She blinked behind thick glasses and looked from me to Mary Ann and back at me again.

"Can we see the denim skirt?" Mary Ann asked, pointing to the mannequin.

The woman nodded. "They're over here."

We followed her as she threaded her way around the racks of clothes. We stopped at a rack of denim skirts. The woman pawed through some skirts on hangers.

"This looks like your size," she said, sweeping a skirt off the rack. She held it up as if she were doing a commercial for denim skirts. "This *is* cute."

"You want to try it on, Lizard?" Mary Ann asked.

I shrugged.

"We'll try it on," Mary Ann told the saleslady.

She took the skirt and led me to the dressing rooms.

"I don't want to buy it," I said.

"You don't have to," she said. "Just try it on. It's comfortable and you'll like it."

I sighed loudly, took the skirt from her, walked into the dressing room, and closed the swinging door.

"Show me when you've got it on," she said.

"Okay."

I took off my shorts and then pulled on the skirt. It didn't look too bad.

"I heard the zip," Mary Ann called. "Let me see."

I opened the door.

She smiled. "That's really cute. How does it feel?"

"Weird."

"How come?"

"It's kind of breezy on my legs," I said.

"I know what you mean. You're just not used to it. But it looks good."

I turned back to the mirror. "Do you think Zach would've asked me to dance if I'd worn this thing?"

"I don't know. But it really looks nice."

"I don't hate it as much as I thought I would." I could only admit that to Mary Ann. She wouldn't tease me.

"How much is it?" Mary Ann asked.

I looked at the tag and showed it to her. "I have that much, plus a couple of bucks left over."

"Why don't you get it?"

I looked at myself again in the mirror. I'd only have to wear it for school dances. The rest of the time it could hang in the back of my closet.

"Okay," I said.

"Good."

I changed back into my shorts and we found the saleslady with the thick glasses.

"We'll take it," Mary Ann said.

The woman took the skirt to the register.

"I'll be right back," Mary Ann said. She disappeared between some clothes racks.

I put my money on the counter.

Mary Ann reappeared and pushed a small package over the counter. "She'll take this, too."

I looked at what she'd handed the woman.

"I don't want panty hose!" I said.

"They're *tights*, Lizard. Just one pair."

"I don't want them!"

"You didn't think you wanted the skirt, either, till you put it on," Mary Ann said.

"No."

"I dare you. You're afraid to take them home."

"Why would I be afraid—"

"Do you want them or not?" asked the saleslady.

"What are you, a chicken?" Mary Ann demanded.

"Okay, okay, I'll take them!"

The woman said, "That'll be another three-oh-nine."

I scowled at Mary Ann and shelled out the money. We walked away from the store, the bag under my arm.

"Thanks a lot," I said. She giggled. "What's so funny?"

"You," she said. "All I had to do was call you a chicken! It was so easy!"

12

I stood in my room wearing nothing but my underwear and stared at the denim skirt hanging in my closet.

Why did I promise Mary Ann that I'd wear it?

"Lizard," Mom called out from the bottom of the stairs. "Better hurry on down to breakfast."

I looked at the clock on my nightstand. I was late!

"Okay," I yelled. "I'll be down in a minute." I went to my drawer and pulled out my favorite pair of shorts.

Then I heard Mary Ann's voice in my head. "I'll wear my denim skirt and tights on

Monday, too," she'd said. "My skirt looks almost like yours."

I dropped the shorts back into the drawer. I couldn't go back on my word to Mary Ann. I'd promised I'd wear the skirt and those ridiculous panty hose.

"Do it!" I ordered myself in the mirror over my dresser. "What are you, a *chicken?*"

I took the package out of my drawer, opened it, and pulled out the panty hose.

"Which side is the front?"

I turned them around and around. I couldn't tell, so I decided maybe it didn't matter.

I sat on the bed and wadded up one leg the way I'd seen my mother do. Then I put my toe in and pulled the hose partway up my leg. Then I did the same on the other leg.

I stood up and grabbed the waistband of the hose and pulled. The top came up partway, but bunches of the legs were still in folds around my knees.

"How the heck do you get these on?"

I grabbed the box the hose had come in and looked at every side of it. *There weren't any directions on how to put them on!*

I pulled the panty hose down partway and tried wadding the top part the way I had the legs. It wasn't easy, but with some wiggling, I finally got them on.

They looked okay but they felt horrible: itchy and kind of clingy and tight.

Then I put on the skirt and a fairly new shirt.

I was ready. Now all I had to do was go to school. I wondered what Zach would say. He'd sure be surprised!

Halfway down the stairs, I stopped.

What was my family going to think? I hadn't worn a skirt since— I tried to think back, but I couldn't remember the last time I'd had one on.

I walked down the rest of the stairs, trying to be very casual, and strolled into the kitchen. I was dying to scratch my legs. How did Mary Ann stand these things?

Mom was standing at the counter pouring a cup of coffee, and Sam and Dad were at the table.

"Morning, honey," Mom said without turning around.

"Morning."

I walked to my place at the table.

Sam looked up and froze for a second, his cereal spoon hanging in midair. His face thawed out in the next second.

"Man, oh man, oh man!" he shouted.

"What?" Mom turned from the counter. Dad looked up from his orange juice.

"Look at Lizard!" Sam said. "A dress!" He hooted and laughed.

My face became really hot. I pretended I didn't care about what he'd said, but I suddenly hated him and wanted to punch his face in.

"That just shows what an idiot you are," I snapped. "This isn't a dress, it's a skirt."

"Lizard's wearing a skirt!" Sam hooted again. "Now I've seen everything!"

My mother looked very surprised. "Honey, when did you get it?"

"Saturday!" I yelled. "Why? Is there something wrong with me wearing a skirt?"

"Well, no," Mom said. "It's just so—out of character for you."

Dad didn't say anything. He just stared at me.

"Call the Channel Nine news team," Sam said, grinning. "They'll want to get this on film."

"What's the matter with you people?" I knew I was screeching, but it was better than crying, and I was afraid I might do something that stupid. "Is it a crime for me to wear something else for a change?"

I didn't give them time to answer. I turned around and ran back upstairs to my room and slammed the door. I pulled off my clothes and threw them on the floor, then put on the shorts that I should have worn in the first place!

"You didn't wear your new skirt," Mary Ann said, standing on the bridge. She was wearing hers.

"I hate it!" I said, stomping past her. "Come on, let's go. We're late."

"But what happened?" she asked, hurrying to catch up. "Why didn't you call and tell me?"

"It was too late," I said. "You wouldn't have had time to change into shorts anyway."

"But Lizard—"

I kept walking. "I'm not in the mood to talk about it, okay? If that's what it takes to get a boy to ask me to dance, well, I just won't go to those dances. It was a stupid dance, anyway. But I don't want to talk about it."

"Okay," Mary Ann said.

"And those *panty hose*! They're impossible to get on, and they feel terrible!"

"I know, but—"

"I don't want to talk about it."

"But you keep talking about it anyway!" Mary Ann said.

We came to a corner and stopped to wait for traffic to pass.

"Did Sam say something?" she asked.

"He thinks he's so smart! I'd like to punch his lights out!"

"Good idea. We'll take turns," Mary Ann said. "First you punch his lights out, then I'll finish him off with karate kicks to the stomach." She kicked her leg as high as her skirt would allow.

We walked along the sidewalk. A couple of older kids rode by on their bikes yelling back and forth to each other.

"Lizard?" Mary Ann said.

"Yeah?"

"I have another idea."

"I don't want to hear it."

"How about if we got you some blush?" Mary Ann said.

"Makeup? No way."

"It gives your skin a rosy glow," Mary Ann said. "Like the way your face looks after you've pitched a no-hitter."

"My face is sticky with sweat after I've pitched a no-hitter."

"Without the sweat," Mary Ann said. "Just glowing and healthy looking."

It seemed dumb to put on something

unnatural in order to look natural.

"I'm not interested."

"Blush would be easier to wear than the skirt," Mary Ann persisted. "Less noticeable."

I sighed. "I s'pose you're going to be on my back till I try it."

Mary Ann grinned. "Right."

"Okay, I'll *try* it," I said. "But if I don't like it, I won't wear it!"

After school, I met Mary Ann by the flagpole.

"Let's go to Whetstone's," she suggested.

Whetstone's Drug Store is on the way home. They have just about everything you could ever want to buy. Their baseball card selection is the best in town.

We pulled open the heavy glass door and walked inside, and that's when I thought of it.

"We can't do this now," I said, stopping abruptly.

"Why not?"

"Because all the kids come here after school. Anybody could come in while we're looking at blush!"

"It's not a big deal, Lizard," Mary Ann said. "Buying blush isn't a crime, you know."

"Yeah," I said, "but if any of the guys come in here, I'll never hear the end of it."

"This'll just take a minute," Mary Ann promised.

She took hold of my arm and steered me to the cosmetics department. I kept checking the aisles nervously. I didn't see anyone, but that didn't mean they weren't there.

Mary Ann stopped at the end of an aisle. "Here's the blush. Let's see what your color is."

I looked over my shoulder. "Just give me whatever you bought. Then let's get out of here."

"Oh, you can't buy just any color," Mary Ann said. "You should buy whatever complements your complexion."

"Whatever." I glanced up the aisle. "Just do it fast."

"Besides, I got my blush at the hair salon," Mary Ann said. "They don't have the same brand here. Now give me your hand."

"What for?"

"So I can look at your skin color."

"It's flesh-colored," I said. "Just like yours. Come on, hurry up."

Mary Ann grabbed my wrist and studied the back of my hand. "Everyone's flesh tones are different."

"Mary Ann, I'm putting it on my face, not my hand."

"It doesn't matter," Mary Ann said. "This is how you check coloring. Here."

She brushed on a little blush from a sampler. "That's pretty good."

I looked up then to see my brother turn the corner and start down the aisle with Stinky.

"Oh, no!" I snatched my hand from Mary Ann and turned my back on the guys. "Let's go!"

"We're not finished . . . "

"I don't care. Let's go!" I dragged Mary Ann into the next aisle. "I don't want them to see us!" I knew the guys were headed for the baseball cards. "Let's stay here for a few minutes."

Mary Ann rolled her eyes but nodded.

After about half a minute, I tiptoed around to peek up their aisle. They weren't there.

I turned back to Mary Ann. "Coast's clear."

"Good," she said. "Let's go back. That shade wasn't quite right for you."

"Just make it snappy."

At the cosmetics section, Mary Ann pulled out another sample. "Let's try this." She brushed a little on my skin.

"There," she said. "See, it blends right into your own skin color."

"Oooo, that's nice, Lizard."

I hadn't heard Sam and Stinky come up behind me. I whirled around to face them.

Sam was grinning idiotically and nodding. "Real nice. Right, Stinky?"

"Riiiiiight," Stinky said. His eyes narrowed and took on a mean glint. I'd apologized to him about the stinko comment, but I knew he was still mad at me. "Lizard in makeup. I wouldn't have believed it in a million years!"

I knew my face was scarlet, and there wasn't anything I could do about it. I tried to calm myself before I spoke.

"Mary Ann wanted to show me the makeup she bought the other day," I said.

"So how come she was putting it on you?" Sam asked. "Maybe she thought it would go with your new skirt?" He looked down at my shorts. "Hey, where's the skirt?"

"Come on," I told Mary Ann. "Let's go."

"Uh, okay," Mary Ann said, "but I have to pay for my new blush."

It seemed to take the guy at the cash register forever to ring up the sale. I prayed we wouldn't run into anyone else we knew.

"I'll never buy makeup again!" I said, once we were finally outside the store. "Not ever in my *whole, entire life!*"

13

It's supposed to give me a rosy glow. I stood in front of the bathroom mirror. *You're supposed to put it on so it looks like you don't have it on.*

I brushed some blush on my cheek.

Mary Ann was right. It was subtle.

It's supposed to make me look the way I do after playing ball, I thought. *Better put on some more.*

I tried it again. That was more like it.

Then I put it on the other cheek.

"More red. Just a little." I brushed it all over my face.

I stood back and looked at myself. That's the way I look after playing a game of baseball.

I went back to my room and hid the blush under my socks at the back of the drawer.

Mom was walking up the hall from her bedroom. "There's some new cereal in the pantry," she said as we passed. "Lizard?"

I turned back.

"Honey, do you feel okay?"

"Sure. Why?"

Mom felt my head. "You look feverish. I wonder if you're running a fev—" She stopped and stared at my face. "Uh—okay, honey." She smiled and patted my arm. "You look nice."

"Thanks."

I started down the stairs with Mom close behind me. I went into the kitchen and pulled a bowl out of the cupboard. Mom sat at the table with Dad and Sam.

I poured the new cereal into the bowl and sat down. Dad was busy eating, but Sam stared at me.

He grinned. "Think you got enough red on your face, Liz—" Mom made a sudden move and Sam yelled, "Ow!" He gave Mom a surprised look, and she glared at him.

Mom must have stomped on his foot under the table. Good for her! Sam's a rat.

Dad sat there, looking from one of us to the other, as if he didn't know what was going on.

Then he stared at me.

I forced myself to sit there for the rest of the breakfast. I ate the new cereal, but I didn't taste it. I just wanted to get it down so I could go back upstairs and wipe the red off my face.

I excused myself as soon as I could and ran to the bathroom.

My face did look awfully red, so I took a piece of toilet paper and rubbed most of the blush off. I left a tiny bit. It looked pretty good, but I was sure no one would know I was wearing it.

Mary Ann said it looked nice when we rode to school with the guys. No one at school seemed to notice I was wearing makeup. Not even Ginger, who usually zeroes in on stuff like that.

At lunch, I sat with Zach and the guys as usual.

"Man, that Tammy Holden's so funny!" Ed said. "Did you hear what she did in Kapp's class?"

Mr. Kapp is one of the science teachers in our group.

"No, what'd she do?" I said.

"She was chomping gum really loud," Ed said. "I could hear her cracking it all the way across the room. So Kapp says, 'Tammy, do you have gum in your mouth?' and Tammy makes this big gulping noise and says"—he put a stupid grin on his face and imitated Tammy's nasal voice—"'Not anymore!'"

I laughed and looked over at Zach. He wasn't even smiling. He was staring over our heads across the cafeteria.

"Earth to Zach," I said.

Zach jumped a little. "What?"

"Aw," Stinky said. "He's thinking about *Lisa.*"

"I was not."

But of course he was.

After lunch when we walked out of the cafeteria, he pulled me away from the others.

"You want to go down to the creek after school?" he said.

"Really?"

"Yeah. We haven't been there in a while."

"Sure."

I smiled to myself. Boys sure could be dumb sometimes, I thought. All it takes is a little blush to get them interested.

I went through the afternoon feeling great. I met Mary Ann after school and told her I was going down to the creek with Zach. She grinned and said she'd see me tomorrow.

I found Zach at his locker. We stopped to

pick up our bikes and rode to the creek.

Zach sat forward on the log, his elbows resting on his knees. He stared into the water and didn't speak for a long time.

"So you like your classes?" he said finally.

That was a funny question. I mean, I see him every day and we'd been in school for over two weeks.

"Yeah. You like yours?"

"Yeah."

"That's good."

I had a feeling Zach wanted to say something, but he just couldn't do it.

"Did you want to talk to me about something?"

Zach looked suprised. "How'd you know?"

I grinned. "I can read your mind."

He grinned back. His ears were turning pink. "Then do you know what I wanted to talk about?"

"No. I'm not getting a clear reading on that."

"Well." He cleared his throat. "You and Mary Ann are really close, right?"

"Yeah."

"Well, do you think—I mean, do you think Mary Ann would mind if I—talk to her?"

Boy, this was really weird. Zach had known Mary Ann as long as I had.

"No. Why would she?"

He reached down and picked a long weed that was growing at his feet. He twisted it around his finger.

"I mean—well, I want to talk to her about—Lisa."

My stomach lurched. I should have known this had something to do with her!

"I'm sure Mary Ann will talk to you about Lisa," I said. "But I don't get it. Why do you need to talk about her with Mary Ann?"

Zach shrugged. "Well, Mary Ann's a girl, and I thought she might know the best way to get to know Lisa."

I stared at Zach. "Mary Ann's a girl? So what am I?"

Zach's ears turned from pink to Cardinals' red. "Oh, yeah. Okay, do you have any ideas?"

"About getting to know Lisa?"

"Yeah."

"Well, what's she interested in?" I almost added, "Besides hairdos and fashion magazines," but I changed my mind at the last second.

Zach thought a moment. "I don't know."

"What is she good at?" I asked him. "Maybe you could compliment her on something she does."

I thought about telling him that Lisa would be dancing the hula at the football game, but I decided he could find that out himself. Why should I help her?

Zach shook his head sheepishly. "I don't know that either."

That's when it hit me. Zach didn't know anything about Lisa.

"So if you don't know her interests or her talents, what is it about her that you like?"

Zach shrugged and laughed a little. "Don't you think she's beautiful?"

"Yeah." My insides ached. "She's beautiful, all right." Would Zach still like her if he knew the truth about her? *Do it,* I told myself. *Tell him what a brat she is!* "But she's not very nice. You should've heard the rotten thing she said to some girls in my gym class."

"What did she say?"

"She said, 'If I were as ugly as you three, I wouldn't want to look in a mirror.'"

"Maybe they'd been mean to her."

"No, they weren't mean at all. She's really awful," I persisted. "And she thinks she's the most beautiful—"

"Lisa is so beautiful, every other girl is jealous of her." Zach cut me off. "Even you!"

I stared at Zach. "I'm not jealous of her. I don't like her because she acts spoiled and mean."

Zach stood up. "I've got to get home. I told Mom I'd help her with yard work."

He was mad, I could tell. "Okay," I said finally.

He started to leave, then turned back. "You're right, Lizard. I should find out more about her. Thanks for the advice. But don't bad-mouth Lisa. It isn't right."

He climbed the side of the ravine and disappeared over the edge.

Good going, Lizard, I thought unhappily.

Another rotten day in a rotten school year. Zach wasn't my buddy anymore and everything was horrible.

I hated middle school!

14

"Stupid hair," I said to my reflection in the bathroom mirror. It wasn't like Lisa's, all full and pretty and falling in thick waves down my back. It hung from my head, a tangled mess.

I pushed a brush through it, and it fell limp around my face.

I sighed. I needed a miraculous makeover like those women in the magazines. Maybe I should have looked more closely at the article at the slumber party, I thought. What could I do with my hair?

Suddenly I realized what I was doing. Wasn't this something all those stupid girly-girls did? Was I getting sucked into The

Change? Would I turn into a zombie like all the others?

I looked into my eyes in the mirror. They still looked the same. I still *felt* like the same Lizard Flanagan.

"Just because you try something different with your hair," I told myself in the mirror, "you're not going to turn into Ginger Flush. Or Lisa St. George. Or any of the squealers."

I looked at my hair again. Maybe I could braid it. It would look more organized that way.

I put it into a ponytail, then braided it to the end.

It didn't look too bad.

Then I put on some blush very, very faintly.

I stood back. That wasn't bad, either.

"Lizard, are you going to hog the bathroom for the rest of the night?" Sam said from outside the door. "You've been in there since supper."

"Just a minute."

I grabbed some toilet paper, wiped my face, then quickly unbraided my hair. I opened the door.

Sam was standing here, glaring at me.

"It's about time," he growled.

"Be sure and shave every bit of peach fuzz from your soft little face," I said.

"Stick it in your ear," he said, and slammed the door.

Sam and I never used to fight or say nasty things to each other. The Change was doing weird things to everybody.

I walked into my parents' bedroom and sat on the bed. I picked up the telephone receiver and dialed Mary Ann's house.

"Hi, Mary Ann."

"What's up?"

"Well, I was just—trying something new with my hair. Do you think a braid would look okay?"

"It'd look nice," she said. "Come over and show me."

"Okay." I hung up.

I told Mom where I was going and sprinted to Mary Ann's house. She was waiting on her front porch. We went upstairs to her bedroom.

"Okay," I said, "go away and I'll call you when I'm ready."

"I'll be right outside the door."

She left and I combed out my hair and braided it in front of the mirror on the back of her bedroom door. Then I put on some blush I'd brought over in my pocket.

It looked as good here as it had at home.

"Okay," I called.

She opened the door and came in smiling. "Turn around." I did a 360-degree turn. "That's nice, but you should try a French braid. It starts high at the back of your head. I read how to do it in a magazine. Want me to try it?"

"Sure, why not?"

I sat cross-legged on the edge of Mary Ann's bed and she stood behind me.

A couple of times I heard her whisper, "Darn!" while she worked, so I figured it was going to look horrible.

Finally she said, "Okay, I'm done. Want to look?"

She handed me a small mirror and I stood in front of her full-length mirror and checked out my hair.

"Hey, you did a good job," I said. "Do it again, and I'll watch this time."

She took the braid out and rebraided it while I watched in the mirror.

I went home and, just for the heck of it, tried to fix the French braid in my hair. I looked in the mirror over my dresser when I was done.

It was pretty messy, but not as bad as I thought it would be.

Someone tapped at my door. "Honey, I have some laundry for you."

"Come on in."

Mom walked in. She stopped in the middle of the room when she saw me, then came closer and looked at my hair.

"Honey, you look very nice with your hair braided."

"Really?"

"Yes, really. I'm sorry about Sam's teasing lately. Don't pay attention to him."

"I know."

Mom put the laundry in my drawer and left. I took the braid out of my hair. Then I took my Cubbies team jersey into the bathroom to take a shower.

I closed the door and went to the bathroom. I looked down at my underwear.

I'd started my period!

Just like that. No gushing of blood, no horrible pains, no embarrassment in front of the class.

"Wow," I said. I felt kind of weird.

I pulled up my shorts and opened the door.

"Mom?" I called. "Can you come up here a minute?"

I felt a little flutter in my stomach. For some reason, I wasn't embarrassed to tell Mom the way I thought I'd be. It was hardly a "celebrate the moments of your life" event, like the commercial says. But I had a weird feeling that I'd remember this.

Mom came up the stairs and I led her into the bathroom.

"I think I started my period," I whispered.

Mom's eyes got big. "I wondered when it would happen. I have just what you need. Hold on."

She disappeared out the door and returned with a blue-and-white box. She opened it and pulled out a white pad.

"I think I know what to do," I told her.

Mom nodded. "How do you feel, honey?"

I smiled a little. "No weirder than usual."

Mom laughed and squeezed my shoulder. "You're growing up, Lizard." She sighed. "So fast." She went back downstairs.

In the shower, I thought about what had happened. I wasn't really different now, but somehow I felt a little bit changed. Not like the girls at school who had gotten goofy and stupid. Just changed. It was weird, but also kind of interesting. I felt more grown up somehow.

Mom came back upstairs to say good night.

"Everything okay?" she asked, sitting on the edge of my bed.

"Yeah. I can feel some of the cramps I've heard about."

"If they get stronger, you can take some Advil." She smiled and kissed my forehead. "Good night, honey."

"Mom?"

"Hmm?"

"Do all women have to wear panty hose?"

"No," she said, still smiling. "Lots of women live in jeans and dress pants."

"Good. Because even though my body's starting to act like it's older, I don't see why I have to make it wear those awful things."

"I don't blame you." She stood up. "Night."

"Night, Mom."

She turned off the light and left.

I stared up into the darkness. I'd gotten my period. I had the feeling I was one of the first girls in my class to have it.

It was hard to believe that I'd worried about it so much. And there was one really good thing about it: I wouldn't have to take a shower in P.E. this week.

I rolled over and snuggled down into the covers.

This was the only interesting thing to

happen since middle school started, I thought. This was one part of The Change that wasn't all bad.

I hoped this was a sign that things would get better.

15

Cramps woke me up a half hour early the next morning. I went into the bathroom and took care of things. Since I was up, I thought I might as well get dressed. I put on my favorite pair of jeans and a red short-sleeved T-shirt.

I stared at myself in the mirror. I sure didn't look any different because I'd started my period. Maybe it was time for a small change. I picked up my hairbrush. It was only six forty in the A.M. I had plenty of time to practice the French braid I'd learned yesterday.

Fixing the braid was easier today. When I was done, I checked myself out in the mirror.

Not bad. In fact, it looked almost as good as

it had when Mary Ann had braided it.

I made my bed, got some Advil from the medicine cabinet, and went downstairs for breakfast.

"Your hair looks nice, hon," Mom commented, pouring her coffee at the kitchen counter.

"Thanks." I slid into my chair across from Dad and Sam. "Hi, Sam," I said. "Like my braid?" I turned my head so he could see.

He looked surprised that I'd asked. "It's all right," he mumbled.

"It's better than all right. It looks good."

My dad laughed. "You tell him, Lizard," he said.

After breakfast I went upstairs and took another look in the mirror.

A ribbon, I thought. *Right at the end of the braid.*

I remembered we had some fabric ribbons in the wrapping-paper box in the hall closet. I pulled out a red one that went with my T-shirt and tied it on.

I brushed on a little blush and stood back.

If someone had told me I looked pretty right then, I might have believed him! "Looking good, Lizard," I told my reflection.

Zach will be surprised, I thought.

Sam and I met Mary Ann at the corner on our bikes. Mary Ann got a big grin on her face when she saw me.

"Turn around," she said. "It looks great!"

"Stinky called and said he had a flat tire," Sam said. "So he and the other guys went to Zach's to blow it up."

I'd have to wait for their reactions to my braid. I figured Ed would either tease or compliment me or both. Stinky was still mad at me, so he'd probably ignore me. I wondered what Zach would say.

After we'd gotten to school and locked our bikes, I pulled Mary Ann aside. "I got my period," I whispered.

"You did?"

I grinned. "It wasn't any big deal. It started kind of slow."

Mary Ann's eyes were big. "What does it feel like?"

I shrugged. "Like nothing. I had some cramps, but they weren't so bad."

"Gee," she said as we headed into the school, "I hope I'm as lucky."

I wondered if Ginger would make a scene over my hair. I didn't see any of them until I got to my locker. Ginger was there. Lisa leaned against the next locker.

I've started my period, I thought, *and they haven't yet.*

I don't know why, but just knowing that made me feel a little superior.

They turned to me.

"Hey, Lizard!" Ginger said. "Great braid!"

Lisa smiled a little but didn't say anything.

"So you think Sam's going to the high school game on Friday?" Ginger asked.

"What about Zach?" Lisa said. "I want him to see me do the hula. I'm going to be dancing out in front of *everybody.*"

"Lisa's going to be the star of the show," Ginger said. "She's the best-looking dancer, so her teacher put her out front."

"I'm sure Zach will go," I said, feeling a little disappointed they didn't say more about my hair. "We always go to the games."

"Great!" Ginger and Lisa grinned at each other.

"Did you tell Zach about my hula?" Lisa asked.

"Uh, no, I guess I forgot." I had no intention of telling him.

"Maybe he already knows," Ginger suggested. "Everybody else seems to."

"True." Lisa tossed her hair. "Everyone's talking about it."

I looked up then to see Shannon, Angie, and Cheryl standing nearby. They were leaning in, listening. Shannon turned and grinned at Angie.

"Oh, get a life, will you?" Lisa snapped at them. "You're such losers, you have to stick your noses into everybody else's business."

Instead of getting mad, Shannon snickered. She and Angie walked away, whispering to each other.

Lisa made a face. "They're such dweebs. I don't know how they can stand each other." She turned to me. "Has Zach ever mentioned my hula?"

"No."

"Well," she said, "I guess I'll have to tell him myself."

"Wait till Zach sees you in that adorable wrap skirt and halter top," Ginger said. "His eyes'll bug out of his head!"

Lisa smiled slyly. "My dance will be just for him."

Oh, boy. I couldn't take any more of this. I pulled out the books I'd need for the morning.

"See you guys." I escaped down the hall.

"Hey, Lizard!" Ed Mechtensteimer stood in front of his locker. "Let's see!" He pointed to his head.

I turned my head so he could see my braid.

He grinned and gave me a thumbs-up sign.

"Thanks!" I called back and continued down the hall.

I found myself looking at the older girls as I walked, the seventh and eighth graders. I bet most of them had started menstruating. It was kind of funny, as if we were all in this secret club together.

The Menstruating Girls' Club. No, make that the Menstrating *Women's* Club.

That's it, I thought. We're different from the girls who haven't gotten their periods yet. The MWC. I wished Mary Ann would get her period so she could join.

At lunch, I sat down at the table with the guys. Zach was talking with Ed and Stinky, so he didn't look over at me right away.

"And then a horde of bumblebees came swarming down on him," Zach was saying.

"Did your uncle live through it?" Ed asked, leaning forward to hear.

"Yup," Zach said. "He dove into the lake, deep, deep down. He held his breath for nearly two minutes."

"Nobody can do that," Stinky said.

"My uncle did," Zach said. "And when he finally came up for air, the bees were gone."

"Wow," Ed said. "He sure was lucky."

"He sure was."

He looked over at me. I turned around to show him my braid. "What do you think?" I said.

Zach grinned. "It looks good on you. Real good."

I grinned back. "Thanks."

Stinky looked at me and scowled but didn't say anything. He looked back at Zach. "So did your uncle ever go into that part of the woods again?"

"Nope," Zach said. "He learned his lesson."

Zach looked over at me several more times during lunch. Each time he gave me a funny smile. I don't mean funny ha-ha. It was a strange smile I'd never seen before.

I wished I knew what he was thinking.

When lunch was over we got up and left. Zach walked out with Ed talking about a science project his class was doing.

I looked over to see a couple of boys, walking down the hall, looking at me. They grinned and mumbled something to each other.

Did I hear the word *cute*?

Me?

Gee, I thought. Maybe this is how Zach feels when Ginger and Lisa look at him. It was kind of weird. I mean it was nice, but it felt funny. I was glad boys don't squeal the way girls do. That would've been really embarrassing.

I thought about that all afternoon. I wasn't interested in having a boyfriend the way the other girls were. I just wanted to maybe dance with a boy once in a while. And beat them in baseball and football the rest of the time.

At least Zach liked my braid. Things were looking up.

16

I love everything about high school football games. I love the crowds, the shouting, the waving, the excitement.

And the music, even though our band is pretty bad.

For this game, I planned to spend halftime getting popcorn and soda. There was no way I was going to watch Lisa the Snot dance her stupid hula.

Mary Ann and I have been to all the high school games for the last three years. We used to go with our parents, but since last year, we've been old enough to go by ourselves.

On Friday night, Mary Ann's father

dropped us off at the game, and we hurried to the gate. I spotted Ginger and Lisa hovering like vultures on the other side of the fence. They were standing at the entrance, eyeing every person who entered. Lisa wore a raincoat over her hula costume. She'd left the raincoat unbuttoned so everyone could see her in it— what little there was of it.

Mary Ann nudged me. "I wonder who they're waiting for?"

"I could never guess. Let's avoid them."

Just through the gate, we walked away from them.

"*Lizard! Mary Ann!*"

We turned and pretended we were surprised to see them. "Oh, hi."

They came trotting over.

"Are the hunks here yet?" Ginger asked.

"If you mean Sam and Zach, I don't know. I haven't seen either of them."

Ginger laughed. "You're supposed to be my spy."

"Spying isn't my style," I told her. "Guess you'll have to keep watching for them."

"Don't worry, we will. We will," Ginger said while Lisa used her eagle eyes to scan the crowd.

Ginger started yakking at Mary Ann then,

but I didn't hear what she said, because I'd just spotted Shannon Bayles. She was wearing a red sweatshirt and leaning against a pole at the back of the bleachers. She clutched a large paper bag and stared at Lisa and Ginger, a smile on her lips. As I watched, Angie and Cheryl stepped out from behind her.

"We found the perfect spot!" Angie said. "Come on!

Shannon snickered. "I can't wait to see the look on her face!"

The three girls turned and headed back under the bleachers.

What was going on? It had to have something to do with Lisa. Something bad they were planning for her.

I wondered if I should follow them and find out.

No, this is none of my business, I decided. Besides, I can't stand Lisa. Why should I help her?

Mary Ann and I made our way into the stands. We have a favorite spot on the fifty-yard line and can usually sit there if we arrive early enough.

Our spot hadn't been taken yet. We sat down.

"Hey, Mary Ann!" a voice called. It was Al

Pickering, sitting with Tom Luther about five rows in front of us.

"Hi!" Mary Ann turned bright red and waved back, smiling. After he'd turned around, she said, "He really is a nice guy."

"I know," I said. "I like him, too."

She nodded, still smiling. "I'm glad."

"We're supposed to do well this year," I said. "Our star quarterback made state—"

"I *know*, Lizard," Mary Ann said. "I still read the sports page."

"And we've got Mike Tanner, one of the best running backs in the conference!"

"We sure do." I could tell Mary Ann was trying not to laugh. Maybe I was kind of excited. I told you I love football.

We sat for a while watching the bleachers fill up around us.

I felt a tug on my braid.

"Well, look who's here!" It was Ginger's voice.

We turned to see Ginger, Sam, Lisa, and Zach sitting in the seats just behind us. It was Zach who'd given my braid a yank. He grinned.

"Hi, guys," I said.

Ginger and Lisa looked like cats who'd just eaten canaries.

"You boys will need to tell us what's going

on," Ginger said to Zach and Sam. "We don't know a lot about football."

You mean you don't know anything about football, I thought.

"Okay," Zach said. "No problem."

"But I'll have to leave when there're five minutes left on the clock," Lisa said. "I have to get ready for my dance."

"Great! I can't wait to see it," Zach said.

I wondered, again, what Shannon and her friends were planning for Lisa. Would they sabotage Lisa's hula? What if they embarrassed Lisa in front of the whole football crowd?

It wouldn't be right, but I wouldn't mind too much. It would be fun to see what Lisa was like when she wasn't cool. "Ooo, I'd be so nervous if I were you, Lisa!" Ginger said. "Don't you just want to die?"

"No, I'm ready," Lisa said. "It'll be fun."

Let her fight her own battles, I thought. *She can take care of herself.*

Just then, our team, the West High Packers, ran onto the field. We stood and cheered. Ginger and Lisa yelled as loud as anybody.

Then we settled down to watch. The Packers won the toss. Our West kicker shot the ball down the field to their thirty-yard line. Their receiver caught it and ran it up ten yards before we tackled him.

"Ooo, Lisa, look at the cheerleaders' out-fits," Ginger said. "Aren't they cute?"

"Yeah," Lisa said. "Maybe I'll go out for cheerleading in high school."

The Packers were back into play. During the next few minutes, Mike Tanner intercepted a wobbly pass and ran it to the fifteen-yard line.

"Man, Tanner's got great hands!" Zach said, leaning forward to Mary Ann and me.

"He sure does!" I said, grinning back at him.

"We're going to have a great season," Sam said.

"I wonder who he'll play for in college?" Mary Ann said.

"I sure hope State U gets him," Zach said.

"They'll recruit him for sure," I said.

"Hey!" Ginger said. "Who're you guys sit-ting with, anyway?"

Zach and Sam sat back.

The players came out of their huddle and lined up on the line of scrimmage. Our quarter-back, Paul Allison, handed the ball off to the running back, who ran it to the ten-yard line and was tackled. It took him a while to get up.

The crowd leaped to its feet, screaming bloody murder.

"Did you see that!" I yelled back at Zach. "He grabbed Jeff Ferguson's face mask!"

"The ref didn't even see it!" Zach yelled, shaking his head.

"Are you *blind*, ref?" I shouted.

"What's going on?" Lisa said.

"One of their players grabbed hold of Ferguson's face mask to tackle him," Zach explained. "That's illegal."

"That's horrible," Lisa said. "What are they going to do about it?"

"Nothing," Zach said. "The ref didn't see it."

"That's not fair!"

Our coach was on the field yelling at the ref and the crowd in the stands was still hollering.

"Let's get the guy a pair of glasses," Mary Ann said to me.

Play resumed with Paul Allison taking the ball over the goal line for a touchdown. An official threw up a yellow flag and gestured an offsides penalty against the other team, but we declined the penalty.

Sam explained what the yellow flag meant to Ginger and Lisa.

"But we should *make* them pay the penalty," Lisa said. "First, the ref didn't see the face mask thing, and now just because we got a touchdown, we're letting them off?"

"But if we accepted the penalty," Zach said, "we couldn't keep the touchdown. What if they got control of the ball?"

"Well," Lisa said, "I don't know, but it seems stupid to let them off so easy."

I looked at Mary Ann, who shook her head in disbelief. Lisa was so dumb!

"Boy, this sure is a slow game." Ginger stood up and stretched. "Hey, Lisa, do you want to go talk to Heather and Sara?"

"Sure," Lisa said. She turned to Zach. "If I'm not back before halftime, be sure to watch for me in the show."

"I will," Zach promised.

"Don't miss us too much!" Ginger said. "'Bye, guys."

Ginger and Lisa made their way down the row, making ten people stand up to let them pass. Then they disappeared up the bleacher steps.

I went back to watching the game and got so involved, it wasn't until the first half was over that I realized that Ginger and Lisa hadn't come back.

"You want some popcorn?" I asked Mary Ann.

"Don't you want to watch Lisa?"

"Are you kidding?"

Mary Ann grinned. "Okay, get us a big tub of popcorn and we'll share."

I turned to the guys. "You want popcorn?"

"Yeah, thanks," Zach said. "But hurry up or you'll miss Lisa."

It took me ten minutes to get to the front of the concession line and buy the corn. I heard the band playing on the field as I loaded three large popcorn tubs into my arms and headed back to the stands.

A flash of red under the bleachers caught my eye. I leaned down and peered between the steps. Shannon Bayles, in her red sweatshirt, was hunched over something. Angie and Cheryl were with her.

Should I sneak up on them to see what they were doing? But if I found out what they were going to do to Lisa, wouldn't I be obligated to stop them?

Yes, I would.

Did I want to stop them from doing something awful to Lisa?

Heck no.

You didn't see them, I told myself. Besides, the popcorn was getting cold. I rejoined the group and handed out the popcorn. Ginger had come back from her social calls and was holding Sam's hand. How could he stand it?

On the field, the band was marching in a ukulele formation, playing "Blue Hawaii."

"And now," said the announcer over the loudspeaker, "join the West High School band and dancers from Diane's Dance Studio in a salute to our fiftieth state, Hawaii!"

It looked like I was going to have to watch Lisa's stupid dance after all.

Nine girls wearing short wrap skirts, halter tops, and leis ran onto the field. Lisa ran down front and center, right in front of the band.

A lot of the guys in the stands whistled and hooted at the dancers in their skimpy costumes. Lisa turned her megawatt smile into the stands in Zach's direction.

"There she is! Isn't she beautiful?" Ginger cried.

"Yeah!" Zach and Sam said at the same time.

They were practically drooling, for crying out loud.

The stands were still half empty because people were getting food. I looked down between the wooden planks at my feet just in time to see Shannon, Angie, and Cheryl. Each of them held a large bulging balloon tied with string. The balloons looked oddly heavy.

Water balloons?

"She'll be purple for months after this permanent dye splashes all over her," Shannon said. "Put on your masks."

The girls slipped plastic dinosaur Halloween masks over their faces. Then they crawled out from under the bleachers in front of the band.

My heart was beating hard and two voices were arguing in my head.

Stop them! They're going to dye Lisa purple! She'll look like a grape! She'll be a laughingstock!

Yes, and it'll be wonderful! She deserves it. She humiliated those three girls in gym class. Besides, you hate her! She's taken Zach away!

Lisa started dancing the hula, swaying her hips back and forth and moving her arms at her sides like waves in the ocean. Guys in the stands whistled and applauded.

Angie and Cheryl were each holding a short wooden pole. The poles were attached to strips of rubber tubing. A pouch tied in between the strips joined the poles together. As I watched, Angie and Cheryl gripped their poles firmly while Shannon put one of the balloons in the pouch.

It was a balloon launcher!

Stop them! Don't let them do this! the voice in my head screamed.

I looked around wildly. Everyone in the stands was watching the hula dancers on the field. No one seemed to notice the three girls setting up.

But I hate Lisa. I hate her! the other voice argued.

Shannon pulled the pouch back, stretching the tubes.

"I can't let it happen, I can't, I can't." I jumped up from my seat and scrambled down between the empty bleacher seats in front of me.

"Where are you going?" Mary Ann called after me.

"What's with Lizard?" Zach asked.

I hurtled over the rail in front of the first row and landed with a thud on the ground about fifteen feet from Shannon and her balloon launcher. The pouch, loaded with the balloon, was pulled back as far as the tightly stretched tubing would allow.

"Let it fly!" Shannon yelled from behind

her mask as she released the balloon.

The dye-filled balloon hurled high through the air.

Lisa, who was concentrating on her dance, didn't see it coming.

Plosh!

The balloon hit the ground close to Lisa's feet and spattered purple inky splotches all over her legs.

She screamed and ran back a few yards. "My legs!" she cried. "Look at my legs!"

Shannon already had put a second balloon in the pouch. She started to pull it back as I raced for her.

"Don't do it, Shannon!" I yelled. *"Stop!"*

I leaped at her and tackled her. She fell like a stone, her mask flying off to the side. She hit the grass facedown with an "Oof!"

Something exploded underneath her.

"Oh, shoot," Shannon said. She slowly sat up and looked at me, blinking.

Her face was a wet, purple mess. The dye covered her neck, chest, upper arms, and most of her hair.

"Oh, wow, Shannon," Angie said, standing next to her, "you'll be purple for months!"

"Shut up, Angie."

I looked up and saw that we were surrounded by football officials.

"Uh-oh," Shannon said.

"Uh-oh is right, kid," the ref said. "You're in big trouble."

I watched the rest of the game with Mary Ann, Zach, and Sam. Lisa had gone home crying that she'd been publicly humiliated and would never dance the hula again. Ginger had gone along to comfort her and to try to scrub the purple spots off her legs.

Everyone pounded me on the back and called me a hero for stopping Shannon from launching any more balloons. Little did they know how much I'd wanted to see Lisa covered with purple dye.

Mary Ann knew, though. She kept looking at me and smiling during the second half of the game. Finally she leaned over and mumbled, "Just think, if your conscience hadn't been working so hard, Lisa would be a purple blob right now."

I grinned at her. "That would've been fun."

"Yeah," she said. "You've changed. Last year you would've let her get splashed."

"Yeah?"

Mary Ann nodded. "But you're more mature now."

"Is that why I had to stop Shannon?" I said.

"Sure," she said.

So that was it. *I'm getting more mature.*

I thought about that on the way home in Dad's car. I rolled down the window and closed my eyes while the fresh September breeze blew on my face.

Maybe Mary Ann is right, I thought. Getting my period, braiding my hair, putting on makeup, and starting middle school were all part of it.

And not letting Lisa get bombed with permanent dye.

It really was sort of miraculous that things like that just happen without your really thinking them out.

Maturity sneaks up on you.

But I couldn't help but feel a little bit wistful. After all, I'd only just started middle school. I'd only had a few weeks to start maturing.

Seeing Lisa covered with ugly, permanent, purple dye would have been *so cool*!

17

I'd just finished reading the newspaper story of the game the next morning when the front doorbell rang.

"I'll get it!" I yelled to Mom, Dad, and Sam, who were still upstairs.

I opened the door and my heart skipped a beat when I saw who was there.

"Hi, Zach."

"Hi, yourself." He stood outside the screen on the front porch. His bike was leaning against the railing. "Thought I'd go to Miller Lake and do some fishing. Want to come?"

"Sure," I said. "I'll get my pole."

I ran up to my room, grabbed my pole and

tackle box, and ran down the stairs again. "Mom?" I yelled. "I'm going fishing with Zach at Miller Lake."

"Okay," Mom yelled back. "Have fun!"

I went out back to the garage, got my bike, and met Zach around on the front porch.

"Ready?" I said. Butterflies fluttered in my stomach a little, and it surprised me. Why was I nervous? This was just Zach. Good old Zach.

"Yep."

We set off on our bikes, our tackle boxes dangling from one hand on the handlebars, the poles dangling from the other.

It felt good to be with him. I figured he wanted to talk about Lisa again. But for now, as we pedaled along, I pretended everything between us was just the way it had been last year.

It took about twenty minutes to get to the lake.

"Want to fish at our spot under the pine tree?" he asked.

"Sure. That's the best place."

He was still calling it our spot. That was nice. I was sure he'd have some places soon that would become his and Lisa's spots, but at least for now we still had our own special spot.

We rode to the tall tree and leaned our bikes against the trunk.

"I got some worms," Zach said.

"Great. They always work better out here than lures."

We got ready and baited our hooks and settled down on the soft grass under the tree.

We didn't say anything for a long time. It was a comfortable quiet. I breathed in the fresh lake air.

"It's a beautiful day," I said.

"The best since school started."

"You have fun at the game with Lisa?" I said. "I mean, before halftime?"

"Oh, sure."

"Good."

"There'll be another game in two weeks," I said. "You can meet her there again."

"Yeah."

There was another long silence.

Then he said, "Lisa isn't really like what I thought."

"She isn't? What did you think she was like?"

"Oh, I don't know," he said. "Remember when we were down by the creek? And you asked me what Lisa's interests were? And her talents and stuff?"

"Yeah."

"Well, it hit me last night," Zach said. "We

don't really have a whole lot to talk about."

"Oh."

"I think I'm tired of her," he said finally.

"Already? How long did that last? A whole week?"

"More." He smiled a little. "Two. Maybe three."

"Oh, well," I said, "there're lots of other girls at school. You'll probably find someone else to like pretty soon."

"Yeah," Zach said. "Someone who likes the same stuff I do."

"Yeah."

There was a long pause. Zach stared at his fishing line in the water and looked very serious.

"Someone who doesn't call other people ugly," he said.

I looked over at him. So he believed me after all.

"Someone who isn't so stupid about football," he said. "So I won't have to explain the game."

I tried not to smile.

"And," he said, "someone who can fish and pitch a no-hitter and has a dog—named Bob."

I started grinning at him. He looked up at

me. He grinned back while his ears turned bright red.

"So shut up and fish," he said.

I laughed. "You know what, Walters?"

"What?"

"I really like what the aliens did to you."

"Huh?"

"Never mind," I said. "Like you said, shut up and fish."

DATE			